The Silent Stranger

A Kaya Mystery

by Janet Shaw

★ American Girl®

Questions or comments? Call 1-800-845-0005,
visit **americangirl.com**, or write to Customer Service,
American Girl, 8400 Fairway Place, Middleton, WI 53562.

Printed in China
15 16 17 18 19 20 21 LEO 10 9 8 7 6 5 4 3 2 1

All American Girl marks, BeForever™, and Kaya®
are trademarks of American Girl.

This book is a work of fiction. Any similarity to real persons, living or dead,
is coincidental and not intended by American Girl. References to real events,
people, or places are used fictitiously. Other names, characters, places, and
incidents are the products of imagination.

Cover image by Juliana Kolesova

The following individuals and organizations have given permission to use
images incorporated into the cover design: northern lights, SurangaSL/
Shutterstock.com; snowy forest, used by permission of
Karen Dingerson Photography; pine cones, Bassarida/Shutterstock.com;
background pattern on back cover, © kirstypargeter/Crestock.

Cataloging-in-Publication Data available from the Library of Congress

To Kathy Borkowski,
historian, with love and gratitude

Beforever™

The adventurous characters you'll meet in
the BeForever books will spark your curiosity
about the past, inspire you to find your voice
in the present, and excite you about your future.
You'll make friends with these girls as you share
their fun and their challenges. Like you, they are
bright and brave, imaginative and energetic,
creative and kind. Just as you are, they are
discovering what really matters: Helping others.
Being a true friend. Protecting the earth.
Standing up for what's right. Read their stories,
explore their worlds, join their adventures.
Your friendship with them will BeForever.

TABLE *of* CONTENTS

Kaya and her family are Nimíipuu,
known today as Nez Perce Indians.
They speak the Nez Perce language,
so you'll see some Nez Perce words
in this book. "Kaya" is short for the
Nez Perce name Kaya'aton'my',
which means "she who arranges rocks."
You'll find the meanings and pronunciations
of these and other Nez Perce words
in the glossary on pages 128–129.

chapter 1

A Stranger with Injured Hands

KAYA STOOD BESIDE Snowbank, running
her hand down the spotted mare's arched neck
and combing her fingers through the black mane
until it lay smooth. Snowbank's heat warmed her
hand, and Kaya rested her cheek against the horse's
shoulder. She was very fond of Snowbank because
the mare had belonged to Kaya's friend and mentor, Swan Circling, who had died last year. Today
Kaya and her people would mark the end of the
mourning period for Swan Circling. A break in the
weather had brought a mild day, so the village was
able to begin the celebration of Swan Circling's life
with a procession. Kaya would ride her own horse,
Steps High, at the head of the procession, leading
Swan Circling's riderless horse.

Kaya closed her eyes for a moment, and an image of Swan Circling came to her. Kaya remembered when a runaway horse had bolted down the valley, with a little baby laced into the *tee-kas* swinging wildly from the saddle. The baby was in danger of being hurt, or killed! Swan Circling had taken a stand in the path of the panicked horse and had raised her arms. Kaya remembered her friend's clenched fists and the fierce look she gave the horse as it bore down upon her. Swan Circling stood her ground, and the horse plowed to a halt right in front of her. She'd saved the baby. Swan Circling was a warrior woman, afraid of nothing. And she had chosen Kaya to be her friend and to use her name when she was old enough.

I will try to be like you, Kaya vowed again to Swan Circling's spirit. *I will be strong so I can help our people as you did.*

As Kaya rested, breathing in Snowbank's good scent, she felt her dog press his nose against her

leg. She looked down. *Tatlo* sat with Kaya's fur-
lined mitten in his mouth, begging her to play with
him. She bent and looked into his intelligent eyes,
stroked his ears, and scratched his broad chest.
"This is no time for games," she said gently, taking
the mitten from him and tucking it into her belt.
He'd been a frisky pup whose curiosity had often
gotten him into trouble, but he'd grown into a
strong, loyal dog who followed her everywhere.

Kaya hung a brightly painted rawhide parfleche
from Snowbank's saddle and laid the reins beside
the saddle horn. Then she carefully draped one of
Swan Circling's dresses across the pommel. Kaya
had already saddled her own horse, Steps High,
and had outfitted her in the fine bridle and grace-
fully fringed saddlebags she'd made. With her
colt, Sparks Flying, at her side, Steps High tossed
her sleek head and nickered, as if to say, "Let's get
going!" Breath from her flared nostrils made white
plumes in the chilly air.

When Kaya had readied both mares, she pulled on her fur mittens again and led the horses up the trail to join the rest of the villagers for the procession. Tatlo followed right at her heels. He sat at her side when she stopped to look out across the winding river that ran between slopes tinted white with frost. This spot had special meaning for Kaya—it was here that she had stood watching and waiting for Swan Circling to return with medicine to save a sick baby. Snowbank had returned with a saddlebag full of medicine but without her rider. Swan Circling had lost her life that night.

Because Kaya was Swan Circling's namesake, it was Kaya's honor to lead Snowbank in the parade. She resolved to do all she could to show her love and respect for her special friend and mentor. *Be with me now and guide me!* she begged Swan Circling's spirit.

As Kaya looked up the valley, she saw three horses come over the rise. Even at this distance she recognized her cousins Raven and Fox Tail, who had been herding horses. Raven was leading an old pack horse, which carried someone huddled in a large bearskin cloak. Several dogs from the village ran out to meet the horses, but Tatlo stayed right beside Kaya. Trying to make out who the slumped rider was, Kaya shaded her eyes. Then, as the riders came closer, the bearskin robe slipped back from the stranger's head. Startled, Kaya saw that the stranger wasn't another boy, as she'd thought, but a woman.

Fox Tail jumped off his horse, the halter rope of the pack horse in his hand. Raven was a little older than Fox Tail and stronger, too. He helped the woman dismount, for she didn't seem to be able to use her hands. She held them crossed on her chest, as though protecting them. Kaya tied Snowbank and Steps High and moved toward the group that had gathered around the stranger.

"I heard the sound of horses," Kaya's blind sister

Speaking Rain said. "Who's here?"

"Raven and Fox Tail, and a stranger," Kaya said softly. "A woman."

"A woman?" Speaking Rain asked. "All alone? What does she look like?"

Kaya studied the stranger. The woman was young, with a broad forehead and dark, arched brows, but her head hung and her shoulders were bent. She glanced around as if she didn't know where she was or how she'd come here. "She's pretty," Kaya said, "but she looks very tired. Her hair is in one thick braid instead of two, like ours, and the backs of her hands are tattooed."

"What's she wearing?" Speaking Rain asked, giving Kaya a nudge.

"Under her bearskin she's got a cape of woven bark with fur at the throat," Kaya said. "She's wearing a necklace of dentalium shells, and abalone ear ornaments, too. She looks like the women who live on the seacoast and come to the Big River to trade."

"*Aa-heh,*" Speaking Rain agreed. "But why would someone from so far away travel into *Nimíipuu* country in the cold season?"

As Kaya gazed at the stranger, the woman tilted her head a little and glanced Kaya's way. Kaya thought she looked sad, and as if she'd like to ask something. But instead of speaking or making a sign, the woman gazed down again at the ground.

The men of Kaya's village were riding into line on the far side of the ceremonial area, but the women and children near Kaya looked curiously at the young woman. Kaya's grandmother hadn't mounted her horse yet, and she took charge, as she often did. She strode between the women on horseback to where the stranger stood. "Good day!" *Kautsa* said in her warm voice. Then with her hands she threw the words in sign language, *You are welcome here.*

The stranger looked into Kautsa's eyes as if she wanted to respond in some way. After a moment, she shook her head a little and looked again at the ground.

"Who is this you've brought to us?" Kautsa asked the boys.

"We don't know who she is," Raven said. "We asked her, but she didn't answer."

"I threw her the words, *Who are your people?*" Fox Tail added. "She didn't answer with signs, either."

"We found her crouched under a hemlock," Raven went on quickly. "Her hands are burned, badly burned. We don't know where she came from or why she's traveling by herself. But we knew she needed help, so I got a pack horse for her to ride."

"She let us help her mount," Fox Tail said. "She wanted to come with us. That's all we know."

"You did well," Kautsa said. "She can't care for herself with her hands like that, and she shouldn't travel alone with deep cold coming soon. You were right to bring her to us." Then she thought a moment before she added, "We need some warm food for our visitor. It will give her strength."

Kaya knew those words were for her. "I'll get a bowl of fish soup," she said.

Kaya hurried to her longhouse and came back with a sheep's-horn bowl of the soup, which she held out to the stranger. But the woman's gaze suddenly fell on Tatlo, who sat beside Kaya. The woman's eyes widened in surprise as she looked at him, and a faint smile came to her lips. When the woman bent and held out her hands to him, Kaya saw that her palms were swollen with blisters. Tatlo sniffed hard at her hands, all the time looking up at her face with his amber eyes.

Kaya spooned a piece of salmon from the soup and held it for the woman to eat. But instead, the stranger gingerly lifted the fish from the spoon with the tips of her thumb and forefinger and offered it to Tatlo. He gulped it down, his tail wagging.

"Surely her people don't feed their dogs before

they feed themselves," Kautsa whispered.

Kaya offered the spoon a second time, tipping it a little so the woman could drink from it. This time she drank the soup hungrily, though her gaze lingered on Tatlo as she ate.

The most powerful medicine woman of Kaya's band, Bear Blanket, made her way through the cluster of people gathered around the stranger. Bear Blanket's face was criss-crossed with deep wrinkles and her hair was thin and gray, but she stood straight and held her head high. Long ago, her *wyakin,* a grizzly bear, had given her the power to heal, and she'd helped many, many people. She gestured toward the stranger's hands and threw her the words, *Are you in pain?*

The stranger lowered her head just a little.

"With her hands like that, she can't speak with signs," Kautsa said to Bear Blanket. "And I don't think she knows our language."

Bear Blanket nodded. *I have medicine that will*

help your hands, she signed to the woman. *Come with me.* Motioning for the woman to follow, Bear Blanket led the way to her longhouse.

The soup must have given the stranger strength, as Kautsa had hoped, for she went with Bear Blanket without hesitation. But as she walked behind Bear Blanket, she looked back over her shoulder, as if she wanted Tatlo to come, too. Kaya wondered why the woman gave her dog so much attention. To Kaya, he was the best dog ever, but there were many good dogs all around, and the woman hadn't glanced at any of them. Kaya put her hand on Tatlo's head to make sure he stayed by her.

Bear Blanket pulled aside the buffalo-hide door flap, and the stranger followed her inside the longhouse. The women and girls began talking about the silent stranger, but Kautsa announced firmly, "Our visitor needs rest now. We'll learn more about her later."

Raven and Fox Tail had been looking on intently. "You two, go get ready!" Kautsa exclaimed to them. "Any time now the crier is going to call for us to start the procession." As the boys ran to their horses, she added in a softer tone, "Kaya, it's time now to finish your preparations."

Kaya took a deep breath to quiet her thoughts so that she'd have a clear heart for the ceremony about to begin. Then she straightened her dress and ran her hands down her moccasin wrappings to be sure they were smooth. She tested the girth on Steps High's saddle, untied the reins, and swung up, taking a firm hold on Snowbank's halter rope. She had only to touch her heels to her horse for Steps High to move forward, her colt right at her side. They took their place at the head of the long line of riders.

When the procession was over, everyone gathered in the larger of the two big longhouses, filling in the spaces all along the sides and around the fires. Shafts of sun slanted through the opening along the ridgepole and touched with light the faces of those around Kaya. Her heart was full as she looked at the men and boys in their deerskin shirts and leggings and their feather headdresses. The girls and women had wrapped their braids with strips of otter fur and had put on their best dresses adorned with elk's teeth. *We are Swan Circling's people,* Kaya thought. *We loved her, and we always will.*

As Kaya went to sit by her sisters, she saw Bear Blanket lead in the stranger, whose hands were now wrapped with soft deer hide. Bear Blanket found a place for the stranger along the wall with other women. *Tawts!* Kaya thought. *Good!* It was the Nimíipuu way to welcome everyone, even an unexpected visitor.

No one had spoken Swan Circling's name aloud since her death, and Kaya's father was the first to say it. "Remember Swan Circling," *Toe-ta* said in his deep voice. "She was a good woman, and a strong one." He went on to speak many words in praise of her, and then he spread his arms wide. "We've shed our tears," he said. "Now it's time to enjoy, and laugh, and feast, and forget sadness for a while! This food the women have cooked is medicine for the heart!"

Kaya's appetite grew as she ate, for all these delicious dishes reminded her of the good things in life. But Kaya saw that the stranger took only a single bite of roasted deer meat, only a nibble of mashed roots cooked with berries. *Her sad thoughts have stolen her hunger,* Kaya thought, and she pitied her.

Since Swan Circling's death, Kaya had woven several small baskets to give others so that she could show her respect for her mentor and her pride in carrying Swan Circling's name. When the dinner was over, Toe-ta asked Kaya to present the gifts that she'd made. As she began to hand out the baskets, Toe-ta said, "We must remember that it's not good for us to mourn alone. We're here to help each other with our grief."

"Aa-heh, tawts," Kaya's mother said, with a glance at Toe-ta. She got to her feet and went to stand by him, for she had something to say, too. "We must remember that it's not good for us to mourn at night," *Eetsa* went on, her cheeks flushed from the fires. "Spirits are very active then and might try to take us away with them. If we're wise, we'll seek help from each other when we're grieving. If we're generous, we'll give whatever help is needed."

As Kaya listened to Eetsa's soft voice, she remembered the many times she'd rested her head on her mother's shoulder and felt Eetsa stroke her hair. Kaya remembered the times Kautsa had held her in her arms when she needed comfort or reassurance. She remembered how Swan Circling had gently smoothed the frown from her face, asking, "Is something troubling you, Kaya?" *I've received much love in my life,* she thought. *That's the real gift I must share with others.*

As Kaya looked from her mother to her grandmother, she caught sight again of the stranger, standing so still and so alone. *Swan Circling would try to comfort her,* Kaya thought, and she was determined she'd befriend the sad woman who had stumbled into their midst.

chapter 2

Many Questions
and a Warning

THE NEXT DAY Kaya's head was filled
with memories of the celebration, but for now the
feasting was over. In the crowded longhouse, life
was back to normal. Men and boys were making
fishhooks, sharpening spears, and crafting arrows
for their strong bows. Women and girls sewed
shirts and leggings of deer hide and wove hemp
baskets. In the cold season, everyone had work
to do.

Kautsa and Bear Blanket were packing pemmican into woven storage bags. Bear Blanket was
older than Kautsa, and they'd known each other all
their lives. They liked to work side by side so they
could talk and laugh together. Eetsa sat with them.
She was sewing moccasins for the twins, Sparrow

and Wing Feather, who outgrew theirs even before they wore them out.

Speaking Rain worked by touch alone, but she was an expert cord maker. She was rolling fine strands of hemp against her leg to make the thin lines the men needed to weave fishing nets. Kaya was stuffing cattail fluff into a hide bag to make a pillow for the stranger. The girls had made their workplace near the women so that they could over-hear everything that was said.

"Her hands are badly burned," Bear Blanket said in a low voice. She glanced over her shoulder at the stranger, who still lay covered with her bearskin at her sleeping place at the back of the longhouse. "They look as though she'd grabbed a burning pole! I put *wapalwaapal* on her hands."

"Aa-heh, your medicine will help her," Kautsa agreed, pausing in her work to push a piece of drift-wood into the red coals of the fire.

"Did she say anything to you while you were

treating her hands?" Eetsa asked Bear Blanket. "Did she tell you her name?"

"She can't—or won't—say a word or give a sign," Bear Blanket answered in a disapproving tone. "After I wrapped her hands, she walked away without even a nod."

"It troubles me that she's traveling alone," Eetsa said. "Why isn't she with some of her people?"

Bear Blanket raised her eyebrows. She was as skilled at anticipating trouble as she was at healing. "Her people might have sent her away from them," she said.

"Sent her away?" Eetsa asked. "But why?"

"As a discipline," Bear Blanket said. "I've lived a long time, and I've known a few bad men, and bad women, too, who have no respect for anything or anyone. Such people need to be banished until they learn respect."

Kautsa frowned. "She doesn't seem like a

bad person to me," she said. "She looks sad, not mean and hurtful."

"Her looks are one thing, but her actions could be another," Bear Blanket insisted, placing a filled bag of pemmican with the other bags to be put into storage.

Kautsa turned to gaze long and hard at the stranger, who was curled on her side. "Hmm, she's barely more than a girl," she said. "If she did a bad thing, I suspect that now she regrets it."

Bear Blanket wiped her hands with some dried bunchgrass. "Aa-heh, perhaps you're right—though this would be your first time!" she teased Kautsa, her eyes twinkling.

Kautsa laughed. Then her brow furrowed again. "She wears a cedar-bark cape from the coast, but a deerskin dress and leggings like a woman from this country," she said. "In my opinion, she could be a slave who escaped over the mountains and is still running. That's why she's all alone."

Kaya shivered. *A runaway slave,* she thought, and she squeezed Speaking Rain's arm. She remembered how enemies from Buffalo Country had captured her and Speaking Rain in a raid and had made them their slaves. If the stranger had been a slave, that could explain why she seemed so sad and troubled.

Bear Blanket closed her eyes for a moment, rocking back and forth as she thought. "There's something I want to tell you," she said. "I had a troubling dream last night. I saw a hawk shooting down from the clouds like an arrow. When it struck its prey, I felt its talons in *my* back!"

Eetsa stopped sewing. Kautsa stopped tying cord around the bag of pemmican. Kaya and Speaking Rain stopped their work, too. They waited to hear what Bear Blanket would say next.

Bear Blanket seized her digging stick and leaned on it so that she could get to her feet. She looked again at the stranger, who was beginning to stir under her blanket. "We don't know who this woman is or how she came here." Bear Blanket kept her voice low, but her tone was stern. "My dream warned me of danger," she went on. "I have a warning for you, too. We must be very cautious until we know if she can be trusted. I'll do what I can for her. Her hands are injured, but I suspect that her spirit has been injured, too. We must watch her very closely!"

Bear Blanket's sharp warning startled Kaya, but no one could question the respected elder's experience or her wisdom. Though Kaya intended to befriend the stranger, she'd do as Bear Blanket said.

"You're wise in these things," Eetsa said respectfully to Bear Blanket. She laid aside her sewing and glanced at the row of fires that ran down the center of the longhouse. Two families shared each fire, and the supply of wood often ran low. "I want to cook some deer meat, but we need more wood," she said.

"We'll get more," Kaya said right away, climbing to her feet. Speaking Rain coiled the length of hemp cord she'd been working on and stood, too.

Pretending to be bear cubs, Sparrow and Wing Feather were growling and wrestling each other on a stack of hides piled up near the doorway. Eetsa gazed at the twins for a moment. "Those bothersome little boys need to play outside for a while," she said.

"Come on, bears. Get your moccasins," Kaya said to the twins. She knew it was hard for the children, so full of energy, to stay inside the crowded longhouse. But the sun shone in a clear sky and there wasn't any wind—the boys could play with their bows and arrows while she and Speaking Rain gathered wood.

Grinning, her little brothers grabbed their moccasins and their antelope hides from a bundle laid against the wall. Kaya and Speaking Rain helped the boys dress themselves warmly, and then they put on their own elk-hide robes and mittens. Outside, Kaya whistled for Tatlo, and he came bounding from the dog pack. As he leaped toward her, he almost seemed to dance with pleasure to greet her. "Fine boy!" she exclaimed. She leaned down to put her cheek to his soft face, then signaled for him to come with them.

They walked quickly on the path that ran along the river, Speaking Rain guiding herself by clasping Kaya's shoulder. The boys ran ahead a little way, frisking with Tatlo, who gave them slobbering licks with his pink tongue. Soon they caught up with Little Fawn and her younger sister, Rabbit, also heading upstream to gather driftwood.

"*Tawts may-we,* cousins," Kaya said.

"Tawts may-we," Little Fawn answered. "Has the stranger finally wakened? Everyone's talking about her. They say she was so tired last night, she could hardly walk to your longhouse."

"Aa-heh," Kaya said. "She was just waking when we came to gather wood."

"Bear Blanket warned us to be cautious until we know if she's trustworthy," Speaking Rain said.

"Others have said the same thing," agreed Little Fawn.

Rabbit leaned close to Kaya and Speaking Rain and lowered her voice. "We think maybe Coyote is playing a trick on us," she said. "Maybe he's disguised himself as the stranger to test us in some way."

"Disguised himself?" Speaking Rain asked.

"Aa-heh," Rabbit said in a hushed tone. "He can take any shape he wants! Remember, he disguised himself as a young man in the story about Warm Weather and Cold Weather? And he turned himself into a baby when he decided to break the fish dam on the Big River. What do you two think?"

Kaya thought a moment about Coyote, always playing tricks and teaching lessons at the same time. "Those stories about Coyote are from long, long ago," she said.

"But he could come back, couldn't he?" Rabbit whispered even more softly, as if the ancient trickster might be hiding right behind the rocks nearby.

Just in case Coyote had overheard and was angry that they were talking about him, Kaya called, "Boys, stay close to me!" They came running back to walk beside her. But Tatlo bounded ahead around the river bend where snow geese were honking, the sounds echoing off the hills across the river.

Then, as if the girls' talk had summoned her, the stranger stepped out of the scrub brush at the river bend. She walked out onto the shore and stood beside the water where a crust of ice had formed on the gray stones. Kaya put her hand on Speaking Rain's wrist, a signal for her to stop walking. The others stopped, too.

"The stranger's up ahead, by herself," Kaya said

softly to her sister. "I don't think she's seen us yet."

Kaya studied the stranger, who stood about the length of a longhouse away. She was shading her eyes with her bandaged hand, looking up as if following the swooping flight of the snow geese. Kaya looked up, too. There, high overhead, a pair of hawks slowly circled on outspread and unmoving wings. Kaya realized it was the hawks that the stranger gazed at so intently. As one of them dived to strike its prey, Kaya remembered Bear Blanket's dream of a hawk that had stabbed her back with its talons.

Tatlo came leaping back down the beach toward Kaya. But when he caught sight of the stranger, he ran to her instead. With her fingertips, she took a bit of food from the bag on her belt and held it out to him. He gobbled it eagerly, then sniffed at her injured hands again. She stroked his head with the back of one hand.

Kaya whistled shrilly. Tatlo glanced her way

but stayed by the woman. Kaya whistled again. Although he usually answered her commands quickly, now he came reluctantly, his tail down.

"I think your dog likes the woman better than he likes you," Little Fawn said. "Maybe she used her power to keep him near her."

"Used her power?" Kaya said. "Why do you say that?"

"We don't know her. We don't know what she'll do," Little Fawn said darkly.

The stranger looked over her shoulder at Tatlo, and then her gaze met Kaya's. The skin under the woman's eyes was bruised with fatigue, and her eyes were swollen. Her hair was loose and tangled, and her lips were dry. She looked as if her long sleep hadn't given her any rest. Still determined to befriend her, Kaya lifted her hand in greeting. But the woman turned to gaze up again at the hawk riding the wind currents high overhead.

Maybe her wyakin is a hawk, Kaya thought. *Maybe*

she's asking her spirit helper for aid. Since the woman wouldn't tell her own name, Kaya decided to call her Hawk Woman.

Little Fawn bent to pick up pieces of the driftwood washed downstream by the river and lodged in the rocks. "Let's stay away from her," she said. "We have work to do."

Kaya gave Tatlo the signal to stay at her side. She and Rabbit began gathering wood, too, piling it at Speaking Rain's feet for her to tie into bundles. Pretending they were hunters, the twins fitted small arrows into their bows and shot them at a knot on a bleached log. When Kaya looked again for Hawk Woman, she had disappeared.

chapter 3

Runs In Circles

ALTHOUGH THE SKIES in Salmon River
Country remained clear, Kaya knew this calm
weather wouldn't last long. Soon winds from the
north would bring snow squalls rushing across
the mountains. She hoped the storms wouldn't
begin before friends and families from other vil-
lages traveled here for the winter Spirit Dances.
This gathering was the most sacred of all, when
her people renewed their bonds with their
wyakins. Kaya longed to take part in the Spirit
Dances, those nightlong gatherings filled with
mystery when wyakins joined their human partners. But before she could do that, she must go
on a successful vision quest and receive a wyakin
of her own.

For some time now, Kautsa had been preparing Kaya for her vision quest. Kautsa had described to Kaya how she would be taken to a sacred place on the mountain and left alone there for several days. During that time Kaya would fast, pray, and wait with patience and strength to meet the guardian spirit that would help her throughout her life. Nothing was more important than making herself ready for that vigil, and every day she prayed she'd be worthy to meet her wyakin when the time came. Until then, she tried to keep her heart clear and to follow the good ways that she'd been taught. And she tried again and again to think how to reach Hawk Woman, who was so lost in sadness, she hardly looked anyone in the eye. *What hurt her so?* Kaya wondered. *Why doesn't our help ease her sorrow in any way?*

Kaya saw that regardless of the suspicions Bear Blanket might have about Hawk Woman, she kept her word to aid her. Each day she placed wapalwaapal on the woman's hands and wrapped them with clean deerskin. Because Hawk Woman couldn't hold a comb, Kautsa smoothed her hair and braided it in the single braid she seemed to prefer. Eetsa gave her finger cakes or roasted camas for a morning meal. Hawk Woman accepted what she was given in silence, with only a glance at her helpers. Then each morning she left the village, going upstream or downstream, or striking off across the valley toward the woods, seeming to search for something. Many saw her go, and everyone respected her need to be alone. But Kaya was very troubled, for Tatlo went with Hawk Woman, trotting at her side as if it was his job to guard her.

One morning Kaya decided to follow Hawk Woman on her solitary walk. She was concerned about her dog and determined to keep an eye on Hawk Woman, as Bear Blanket had warned. Kaya took the trail that ran up to the ridgeline. Hawk Woman and Tatlo hadn't been gone long, and Kaya

was sure they'd headed this way, but they weren't
in sight. She walked faster and left the trail so that
she could gain the ridge more quickly.

As Kaya made her way along the hillside, she
came upon the enormous paw prints of a wolf. She
knew wolves came into the valley to hunt the deer
and elk driven down by deep snow in the mountains. But these wolf prints surprised her, for they
were larger than any she'd ever seen. She knelt
and placed her palm in one of them. The print was
larger than a man's hand. Kaya followed the wolf
prints for a little way. Where the wolf had crossed
a rocky stretch, she lost its trail, but soon she saw
both elk and deer tracks. This area was a crossroads
for many animals.

Although there was no wind, Kaya saw bunchgrass shake and quiver. Were the Stick People
crossing here, too? She'd never seen them, but all
her life she'd heard stories about the little spirit
people. She knew that sometimes they played tricks

on humans, and sometimes they offered help—and she knew that they became angry if they weren't thanked with a gift for the help they gave.

Then she spotted a dog's prints on the frosty ground, and the print of a patched moccasin—Hawk Woman's. As Kaya followed the tracks, she saw where the dog had chased a rabbit and where the woman had sat on a frost-covered rock. Then Kaya rounded an outcropping and caught sight of Hawk Woman, standing on a promontory over-looking the river. Her head was lifted. She was watching a hawk that circled overhead, sunlight glinting on its wings. Though she hadn't spoken even a single word to anyone in the village, she was murmuring something to Tatlo, who sat gazing up at her, his ears pricked in attention.

Kaya stood still. She heard the caressing sound of Hawk Woman's voice, and now she understood that the woman was singing. But what was the song? Did it give her power over Tatlo, as Little

Fawn had said? Then Kaya realized that Hawk
Woman wasn't singing to Tatlo after all—she was
singing to a doll she'd tucked into her belt. As she
sang, she stroked the tattered doll with the back
of her hand. Kaya listened uneasily to the gentle
lullaby. Why would a grown woman sing to a doll,
as if she were still a child?

Listening intently to Hawk Woman's voice,
Tatlo hadn't even noticed Kaya's approach. As
she watched her dog, Kaya remembered him as a
puppy. She'd first seen him in the den that Lone
Dog had dug for her pups in a hillside. He was
the only male of the litter, and he'd been so plump
that he looked like a ground squirrel, so Kaya had
named him "Tatlo." Now, as if he felt how much
she loved and needed him, he turned and looked
her way.

Kaya whistled. Tatlo glanced again at Hawk
Woman, then trotted to Kaya and sat at her feet.
She took his face in both hands, looking down into

his warm, wise eyes. "Why do you leave me now?" she whispered to him. He licked her cheek, whined low in his throat, and licked again.

Hiding the doll under her bearskin cloak, Hawk Woman followed Tatlo. She halted in front of Kaya and pressed her lips together. Tears stood in her eyes as she held out her bandaged hands and turned them palms up—empty.

Confused, Kaya threw her the words, *What are you searching for? Tell me. I can help you find it.*

Hawk Woman shook her head. She wouldn't— or couldn't—tell Kaya anything. After a moment, she walked back to the trail and started downhill.

"Stay with me," Kaya told Tatlo. She put her hand on his head. But he looked anxiously at Hawk Woman and loped after her instead, catching up to her as she went over the top of the ridge. As Kaya watched him go, she felt a stab of frustration with Hawk Woman, and a stab of longing for her dog. Then she had an idea how she might reclaim him while still giving Hawk Woman the friendship she needed.

Back at the longhouses, Kaya looked over the many dogs that guarded the village. Some slept, curled up with their noses tucked under their tails. Several dogs played chase on the brushy slope nearby, and some pups fought over a well-chewed bone. The big black leader of the dog pack got to his feet when Kaya approached. But it wasn't the pack leader that Kaya wanted—she was looking for one of Tatlo's littermates, a female called Runs In Circles, because as a puppy she'd chased her own tail.

Kaya found Runs In Circles sleeping in a sunny spot between the longhouses. She had a light brown coat and a pale muzzle much like Tatlo's. Although she was a little smaller and not as confident as her brother, they were both strong, good-tempered dogs and eager to please. Runs In Circles lifted her head, then rolled onto her back when Kaya scratched her chest. "Good girl," Kaya said. "I need you now. Will you come with me?" She slipped a rope around the dog's neck so that she could lead her.

Kaya met Hawk Woman and Tatlo coming back to the village on the trail from the ridge. When Tatlo spotted Runs In Circles, he ran to greet his sister, sniffing her, his tail wagging. "Stay with me," Kaya commanded him again. But instead, he bounded back to Hawk Woman, and Kaya heard her whispering softly to him.

Kaya waited until Hawk Woman came up to her, and then she threw her the words, *I am your friend, and here is another friend for you.* She held out the rope she'd put around Runs In Circles' neck.

Hawk Woman looked down at Runs In Circles. The dog's brown eyes were on her, and her bushy tail was wagging.

When the woman looked up again, Kaya threw her the words, *She's a good dog. Do you like her?*

Hawk Woman frowned, as though troubled by Kaya's question. Then she shook her head and started to walk on. But Kaya stepped into the center of the path and offered Runs In Circles' rope again. *I need my dog,* she signed. *Please take this one instead.*

Hawk Woman's brow furrowed as she considered what Kaya had told her. Then her eyes widened in alarm. She bent and put her arm around Tatlo's neck, holding him closely against her side. Clumsily, she turned her right hand back and forth, making the sign for *No!* Gritting her teeth, she shook her head again. Hawk Woman wanted only Tatlo, who stayed at her heels as she walked on down the trail.

Kaya's chest was hot with troubled feelings. Her intention was to help Hawk Woman, as she was certain Swan Circling would, but the woman ignored her offers. *And when I begged to have my dog back, she refused me,* Kaya thought. *Is she the kind of person Bear Blanket warned us of, one who has no respect for anything or anyone?*

chapter 4

The Tattered Doll

IN HER SLEEP Kaya dreamed that she was
swimming up through deep, dark water. At last she
reached the surface and pulled herself up onto the
riverbank. But right in front of her, coiled on the
stones, a rattlesnake lay waiting to strike her! She
heard someone saying her name and she woke with
a gasp. Speaking Rain, lying beside her under the
warm buffalo robe, was whispering, "Kaya, Kaya!"

Kaya blinked at the dim longhouse lit only by
banked fires, their soft light reflecting on the tule
mats. Along the walls other families slept under fur
blankets, the little boys sleeping between the fires.
She rubbed her eyes and took Speaking Rain's hand
in hers. "I dreamed a rattlesnake was about to bite
me!" she whispered.

"I heard you moaning," Speaking Rain said. "Hawk Woman's moaning, too. Do you hear her?"

Kaya listened. She heard wind whining around the longhouse and trees popping in the cold. She heard a burning stick break with a crackle of sparks. Then she heard a sound like water sighing over rocks. She rose to her elbow and looked at the place at the back of the longhouse where Hawk Woman slept. She was turning and twisting under her bearskin.

"She's been thrashing around as if she's try-ing to get away from something," Speaking Rain whispered.

Kaya sat up so that she could see better. Hawk Woman had seemed increasingly troubled as she searched in vain up and down the valleys, and nights gave her no rest. She fell asleep when every-one else did, but after a short while bad dreams seized her. She struggled as she tried to escape them. Usually she quieted after a time, and Kaya hoped she'd settle down again now.

But as she looked, Hawk Woman pushed off
her bearskin and got to her knees. She grabbed her
cedar-bark cape and pulled it on over her head as if
it were morning, though Kaya could see the moon
through the opening along the ridgepole and knew
that sunup was still a long way off. "I'm going to
see if I can help her," Kaya whispered to Speaking
Rain. "Maybe her stomach is sick and she needs to
go outside."

Slinging a deerskin over her shoulders, Kaya
crept around the fires to where Hawk Woman
knelt. When Kaya got closer, she realized that
although Hawk Woman had dressed herself, her
eyes were closed. She was acting in her sleep, like
a sleepwalker. Moaning, she cradled her little doll
in her arms and rocked back and forth.

Kaya went down to her knees and touched
the woman's shoulder. But Hawk Woman didn't
respond. Kaya squeezed her shoulder this time.

Still Hawk Woman bent over her doll, dragging up deep sighs.

Bear Blanket came and bent at Kaya's side. "She woke me, too," she whispered. "Let's help her lie down again."

Kaya moved aside to let Bear Blanket put her hands on Hawk Woman's shoulders and guide her back to her bed. Then Kaya tried to take the doll from her so that they could pull up the bearskin again. But Hawk Woman hugged her doll to her chest and began to fight them, lashing out with her legs. She twisted and kicked, catching Bear Blanket in her stomach with a foot. Bear Blanket doubled over, gasping. Kaya grabbed Hawk Woman's ankle as tightly as she could, but Hawk Woman leaned forward and bit Kaya's arm—like a rattlesnake! Kaya didn't make a sound. She knew the woman was fighting in her sleep—she needed to wake her somehow, so she pinched her cheek. Hawk Woman only kicked harder.

While they struggled silently, Kaya remembered how Hawk Woman had sung a lullaby to her doll. Would a gentle song calm the woman? Kaya released her grip on Hawk Woman and began to sing a lullaby she'd learned from Kautsa. *Ha no nee, ha no nee,* Kaya sang softly. As she sang, she stroked Hawk Woman's shoulder, patting her as a mother comforts a child.

As the lullaby entered her dream, Hawk Woman stopped struggling, and her face relaxed. Gently Kaya urged her to lie down again, and after a little while Hawk Woman lay on her side, curled around her doll. Kaya knelt there a little longer, stroking Hawk Woman's shoulder until her sighs evened out. "Poor woman," she whispered to Bear Blanket.

"Waking or sleeping, she's tormented," Bear Blanket whispered, "but I think we can go back to our beds now."

Kaya crept back to her sister and slipped

underneath their buffalo skin again. "I don't hear her moaning anymore," Speaking Rain whispered.

Kaya listened hard, but she heard only an owl hooting nearby and a coyote's shrill howl from across the valley. "Sometimes she's as gentle as a child, but she can be as fierce as a cougar!" Kaya whispered, her lips close to her sister's ear. "She's like two women sharing one body."

"Light On The Water needs to stretch her legs," Running Alone said with a smile. The young mother held her little daughter's chubby hand in her strong one. The child wore a deerskin dress with rabbit-fur leggings and fur-lined moccasins to keep her warm. Running Alone had wrapped a small deer hide around her daughter's shoulders, too. On her back, Running Alone carried a tee-kas with her new baby laced snugly inside the buckskin wrapping. Kaya heard the baby begin to fuss.

"I'll look after Light On The Water," Kaya said, bending to kiss the little girl's plump cheek. "She's a precious one, isn't she!"

"Watch out for her," Running Alone cautioned. "She's learned to run fast, and she often runs *away* from me."

"I'll keep her near me," Kaya said. Troubling images from the long night stayed with her, but her spirits were higher now that she was busy again. She led the little girl outside, where other children were playing with small tepees and stick horses they'd made.

High, thin clouds signaling a change of weather stretched across the sky. The chill air felt charged with anticipation, for everyone except the youngest children was busy with preparations for the coming Spirit Dances. Many families and friends would journey here shortly, swelling the size of the village. For some time the women had been cleansing themselves to prepare for the sacred ceremonies and had been cooking for the feasts. Both the women and the men had been readying gifts to share at the give-away. A pile of neatly stacked lodgepoles was waiting at the side of the clearing, for soon the women would put up another longhouse large enough to hold everyone for the ceremonies, which would go on for several nights.

Kaya guided Light On The Water to the stack of poles piled waist-high. Some were freshly cut, and the scent of pitch was strong. Light On The Water wrinkled her nose when Kaya sat her on a pole at the bottom of the stack. "You stay put," Kaya told her. "I'm going to get a piece of hide so I can make a little tepee for you to play with."

Not wanting to leave Light On The Water alone, Kaya glanced around. She saw Hawk Woman working only a short distance away. With Tatlo sitting at her side, she was shaking powdered cedar onto her bearskin to keep away fleas.

Just then, Hawk Woman looked up, and her
gaze fell on Light On The Water. Her stern expres-
sion softened a bit, so Kaya tried again to reach her
by throwing her the words, *Isn't she a pretty girl?*
Hawk Woman nodded slightly but returned to her
work. After a moment, Kaya hurried back to their
longhouse for a scrap of deer hide.

Kaya quickly found a bit of hide, but when
she got outside again, she saw that Light On The
Water, instead of sitting quietly, had climbed to
the top of the stacked-up poles. As Kaya hurried
over to lift her down, the little girl took a step
backward, lost her balance, and sat down with
a thump. Suddenly all the poles were in motion,
rolling one after the other. With a cry, Light On
The Water fell backward, the poles cascading
beneath her. Kaya ran.

But Tatlo ran faster! As Light On The Water
tumbled, he raced forward and grabbed her dress
in his teeth. Backing up, he dragged her out of

the path of the slide. She sat bawling until Kaya grabbed her up and held her close. Kaya wiped tears from the child's cheeks. "You're all right!" she said. "Tatlo took care of you. Look, he's wagging his tail. He knows he did something to be proud of!"

As other children came running to see what had happened, Kaya realized that Hawk Woman was still standing by the bearskin. Her lips were parted, her eyes wide with alarm, but she stood as if frozen in place. *Why didn't she keep an eye on Light On The Water?* Kaya thought. *She doesn't care about anyone else, not even a little girl!* Anger was a bitter taste in her mouth, and she tried to calm herself.

Hawk Woman dropped the pouch of powdered cedar and rushed to the doorway of the longhouse. She looked back over her shoulder fearfully, and then the buffalo-hide door flap swung closed behind her.

After Kaya returned Light On The Water to her
mother, she picked up Hawk Woman's bearskin,
slung it over her arm, and went into the longhouse.
She found the woman kneeling by her sleeping
place, shoving her doll under her bedding. Still
fighting to be calm again, Kaya held out the bearskin to her.

Instead of taking it, Hawk Woman buried
her face in her hands. Every line of her hunched
shoulders and her bowed head seemed to say
Leave me alone! Without meeting Kaya's gaze, she
got to her feet and went outside. Kaya followed.
With a low whistle Hawk Woman called Tatlo to
her. Walking fast, she left the village on the path
that led to the river.

Kaya watched her dog as he trotted willingly
at Hawk Woman's side. He had no fear of her.
But Kaya was very troubled as she wondered
what thoughts whirled in the woman's head.
Why would she run away from a crying child?

Why had she wanted to hide her doll?

Only a few women were in the longhouse, and they were busy with their cooking. Kaya went to Hawk Woman's sleeping place, searched underneath the hides for the doll, and pulled it out, laying it on the bearskin. With her fingertip, Kaya touched the doll's necklace of shells, so like the one Hawk Woman wore. She traced the beads that adorned its deerskin dress, and the single, wispy braid of horsehair that fell over its shoulder. Large eyes and curved lips had been painted on its face. Kaya could see that the doll maker had given it much time and care and had used her skills well. But now it was worn and dirty, deer-hair stuffing leaking out its seams. Its pretty face and its arms were black with soot.

Kaya carefully placed the doll back underneath the bedding, where Hawk Woman had hidden it. Then she sat a moment, lost in thought. Had Hawk Woman's mother made the doll for her when she was a child? Did it remind her of her home far away? Why else would an old tattered doll mean so much to a grown woman?

chapter 5

Danger for a Dog

NOW DEEP WINTER had settled in.
Although the morning was sunless and achingly
cold, Kaya and the others bathed in the river so
that they'd be clean and strong, both in body and
in spirit. As Kaya walked with the other girls on
the path back to the village, she felt the shock of
the wind on her wet face as she turned to look
upstream. Her heart sank when she spotted Hawk
Woman walking off alone again, with Tatlo at her
side. *I wish she had never come here!* Kaya thought.
That ungenerous thought shamed her, so she said
loudly enough for the others to hear, "I hope she
finds what she's searching for."

When Kaya reached the longhouse, Kautsa was
waiting for her, several large gathering bags over

her arm. "Kaya, do you remember that story about how Coyote caught his braid in a tree and had to cut it off to get loose?" Kautsa asked.

"Aa-heh, I remember," Kaya said. Many times her grandmother had told how Coyote had gone traveling with his little son, giving the pup a ride on his back when he got tired. Coyote was climbing a tall tamarack when he heard his son crying down below. When Coyote tried to jump down to help him, Coyote's long braid caught on a branch and wouldn't come loose. Coyote swung there, helpless to go to his son's aid. He had to take his flint knife and chop off his braid in order to free himself and tumble out of the tree. When he looked up, there was his long black braid still hanging from the branch. He vowed that his valuable hair wouldn't be wasted, so he made it into tree moss for the people to eat. "He turned his braid into good food for us," Kaya said.

"What a smart girl you are!" Kautsa said with

a smile, handing her the hemp bags. "I need to cook more *ho'pop* for our visitors for the Spirit Dances. We want to have plenty to offer at the feasts! The black moss here in the valley isn't as good as that in the mountains, but it will have to do. Go with Little Fawn, and get your horses. A good gathering place is up the valley where the tamaracks are thickest."

As Kaya set off to find Little Fawn, her thoughts went back to Hawk Woman, for she'd been heading toward the wooded hills Kautsa was sending them to. This could be another chance to see what the woman did on her wanderings.

Steps High and Little Fawn's gray mare were in the horse herd not far from the village. As the girls got their saddles and walked in the direction of the herd, Runs In Circles came bounding after them. Kaya stopped to scratch the dog's ears and felt her warm breath on her face. "Are you asking to come with us?" she asked, and Runs In Circles jumped against her leg with excitement.

"That dog thinks you need her, now that Tatlo belongs to Hawk Woman," Little Fawn said. Her eyes narrowed, and her lips puckered as if she'd tasted something sour.

"Tatlo doesn't *belong* to Hawk Woman," Kaya said stubbornly.

"She acts as if he does," Little Fawn insisted. "Hawk Woman is like a baby that grabs anything she wants."

"It's true she can be like a child playing with her doll," Kaya admitted.

"And who knows what she'll want next?" Little Fawn said. "It might be your pretty horse she'll use her power on, Kaya."

"Why do you say that?" Kaya asked with a frown.

"As the Spirit Dances near, spirits come closer and grow stronger," Little Fawn said. "Maybe Hawk Woman's powers are getting stronger, too."

Kaya tried to ignore her. Would Hawk Woman really try to claim Steps High? Or was Little Fawn only teasing, as she often did?

"Did I make you frown?" Little Fawn asked.

"I didn't sleep well," Kaya said. "I had a bad dream, and Hawk Woman wakes us every night with hers."

"I had a troubling dream, too," Little Fawn said. "Until that woman came, we seldom had bad dreams. I think she brought them with her."

When the girls reached the top of the rise, Kaya saw the herd grazing on the far hillside. There were brown and black horses, whites and grays, too, and many of the spotted ones that Kaya liked best. The horses flicked their ears toward the girls as they walked closer.

Kaya whistled for Steps High and she left the herd, her colt Sparks Flying trotting right at her heels. The colt was growing quickly, but he still stayed near his mother. Steps High pushed her head affectionately against Kaya's chest as Kaya stroked her horse's smooth muzzle. "Tawts may-we, beautiful one," she murmured as she slid a rope bridle onto her horse's lower jaw. "You'd never be anyone's horse but mine, would you?"

Little Fawn quickly got her mare, too. The girls saddled their horses and hung the gathering bags over the saddle horns. Then they swung up, turning the horses toward the wooded slopes at the far end of the long valley.

As Kaya rode, the heavy thoughts that weighed on her began to lift. She rejoiced to be up on her spirited horse, who pranced and snorted and tossed her head with pleasure. She delighted in Steps High's easy gait as they cantered along, and she saw that the sour look had left Little Fawn's face. Now and then, Sparks Flying kicked up his heels as small birds rose around the horses' hooves and flew off in a burst. Runs In Circles leaped after the birds, then came charging back to join them

again. Kaya thought only one thing would have
made the ride better—to have Tatlo running at her
side, too.

After a time they reached the slopes where
the frost-covered pines and tamaracks made a
silver-green tunnel. They rode through single file,
ducking under overhanging branches. The light
here in the woods was dim. Kaya rode in the lead,
peering down at the trail. She didn't see footprints,
but she did see faint scratch marks at the base of
a hollow tree—maybe the Stick People had taken
shelter there. A little farther along the trail, she
saw deer droppings that a dog had rolled on. She
smiled to herself, thinking that if Tatlo was nearby,
she'd smell him before she saw him.

Little Fawn reined in her horse and pointed
at the canopy of tamarack branches overhead.
"There's the moss we're looking for," she said.

Kaya looked up. Dark moss hung from the
branches like strands of long black hair. Kautsa

was right—this was a good place to gather it. Kaya dismounted and tied Steps High's reins to a tree. Sparks Flying nuzzled at his mother. Kaya took a few rose hips from the bag she wore at her waist and scattered them in gratitude for the food they were taking. Then she climbed onto her horse's back and stood on Steps High's rump, reaching up to pluck moss from the tree branches.

Little Fawn dismounted, looped her mare's reins around a branch, and picked up a long stick. Then she climbed up to stand on her horse's rump, too, so that she could pull down the moss that hung from the higher branches.

Sniffing excitedly, Runs In Circles ranged back and forth across the trail ahead. "She might have Tatlo's scent," Kaya said as Runs In Circles loped off through the woods. "I saw Hawk Woman coming this way."

The moss was lightweight, and it took many, many handfuls to fill a bag. Kaya was absorbed in the work when suddenly the horses began to shift about nervously, tossing their heads and pulling at the ropes that tethered them.

Kaya looked up quickly and jumped off her horse. Little Fawn stopped work and jumped down, too. They listened. "Where's Runs In Circles?" Kaya asked in the silence. "If the horses are frightened, she should be growling."

"She didn't come back," Little Fawn said.

Kaya felt her heart thud in her chest, and she put her hand on Steps High's neck. She peered into the woods and up into the trees, but saw nothing.

Then the gray mare reared, her nostrils flared and her eyes wide with alarm. The branch she was tied to snapped off. Little Fawn leaped to grab the reins, but her horse bolted down the trail back toward the valley.

Steps High tossed her head, trying to flee, too. But Kaya had tied her rope tightly to the hemlock, and Sparks Flying nosed up against his mother's flank—he wouldn't leave her.

"My horse will run back to the herd," Little Fawn said. "We'd better look for the dog."

Walking silently, Kaya followed Little Fawn deeper into the pines. A short way off the trail, they came to a small clearing ringed with dark hemlocks. Little Fawn stopped and held up her hand, warning Kaya not to go further.

Kaya craned her neck to see past Little Fawn, and her heart beat faster. There in the clearing, a large cougar crouched over a bloody animal that it had killed. The unfortunate animal was light brown—a small deer, perhaps. Or a dog?

Has the cougar killed Tatlo? Kaya thought with horror.

But even as that thought came to her, she saw Tatlo, followed by Hawk Woman, come out of the woods on the far side of the clearing. Tatlo's hackles were raised and a low growl came from his throat.

Hair bristling, muscles bunched, the big dog poised himself to attack the cougar. In another breath, Tatlo was rushing forward, showing tooth and fang, his fierce growl full of menace as he charged at the cat.

For a moment the cougar hesitated, not wanting to give up its kill. But as Tatlo charged on, the cat leaped up into a hemlock like a brown shadow. Snarling defiance at the dog, it peered down, its eyes yellow slits. Then it leaped to another tree and disappeared.

Only then did Kaya realize that the bloody creature lying in the clearing was Runs In Circles. She caught her breath, sorrow stabbing her. "Poor dog!" she cried.

Tatlo went on stiff legs to his downed sister. Tail lowered, he sniffed her body from nose to flanks, then lifted his head in a howl that echoed through the woods.

A sudden gust of wind shook a curtain of frost

from the hemlock branches. As Kaya brushed it from her face, she squinted through the dim light at Hawk Woman, who was gazing intently at Kaya and Little Fawn. Her brow was furrowed and her lips parted. Then she glanced down at Runs In Circles' body. Her face, shadowed by her bearskin, revealed no emotion. A moment later, she turned away as if impatient to get back to her search. Tatlo hesitated only a moment before following at her heels, leaving Kaya and Little Fawn alone in the clearing.

"She slipped away like a snake!" Little Fawn hissed.

Kaya remembered her dream of the rattlesnake poised to strike her, and she shuddered.

"You told me she didn't like Runs In Circles," Little Fawn said darkly. "Maybe she used her power to get rid of her. And she likes Tatlo now, but what if she turns against him? Would she bring him harm? Would she harm us?"

As Kaya thought about Little Fawn's words, she
felt fear growing in her. Perhaps Little Fawn was
right—the woman was dangerous, killing anything
she chose. Did she have the power to summon evil
spirits to the Spirit Dances if she chose to? Kaya
closed her eyes, searching herself for answers. *Help
me understand, Swan Circling!* she silently begged her
friend's spirit.

chapter 6

Little Questions and Big Questions

THE NEXT DAY, Kaya worked with the other girls and women to put up a large longhouse for the all-night Spirit Dances gatherings. They raised a big frame of lodgepoles and spread several layers of tule mats over it. Then they laid other poles on top of the mats to keep them from blowing away, for a strong, gusting wind had come up, spitting snow from ragged clouds.

As Kaya worked, she prayed silently, *Creator, help me face life with a strong will and without fear of any creature or any person.* She wanted to keep her heart free of bad feelings about Hawk Woman so that she wouldn't taint this lodge they were building. It was a sacred space, and soon many powerful spirits would enter it. Kaya imagined that even now the spirits were coming closer, just as groups of family and friends were on their way here to join them.

But when the new longhouse was completed and she'd gone back to her own, Kaya felt she should speak about her worries to Kautsa. Kaya knew she could always turn to her wise grandmother for comfort and guidance. She found Kautsa unpacking her special dress and the belt decorated with quillwork that she would wear for the gatherings. Kaya knelt at her side and touched a blue stone bead with her fingertip.

Kautsa glanced up at her. "You're frowning, granddaughter. Is something on your mind?"

"I think I have a question for you," Kaya said.

"It seems to me that 'I have a question for you' were the first words you learned to say," Kautsa said with a smile. She was straightening the long fringe on the sleeves of her deerskin dress and checking to make sure that the many elk teeth were sewn on securely. "Tell me what you'd like to know."

"I want to ask you—" Kaya hesitated. "I have too many questions. I don't know which one comes first."

Her brow furrowed, Kautsa gazed closely at Kaya. "You're carrying a heavy weight, aren't you?" she said. "Why don't you begin with a little question, one small enough to hold in the palm of your hand."

Kaya smiled. She held out her upturned palm. "Here's a little question, then," she said. "You've heard Hawk Woman crying in her sleep, haven't you?"

Kautsa nodded. "Aa-heh, I think you know the answer to that one," she said. "We've all heard her. And I've also heard you get up and go to her, as I have from time to time."

"Her dreams frighten her," Kaya said, "but she fights us when we try to waken her." Kaya sat and settled a little closer to her grandmother's side.

Kautsa raised her eyebrows. "You know that no one is responsible for what she does in her sleep," she said.

"Bear Blanket had a troubling dream," Kaya said. "I had one, too, and so have others. Little Fawn says the bad dreams come from Hawk Woman."

Kautsa pressed her lips together. Then she said, "What do you think, Kaya?"

Kaya thought a moment, studying her grandmother. Kautsa's black hair was threaded with strands of gray, and deep lines fanned her eyes. "You've told me that dreams come from many places—some are visions, some are warnings, some are memories," Kaya said. "But I think our dreams belong to us, not to Hawk Woman."

Kautsa put her hand on Kaya's knee. "I think so, too," she said.

Kaya thought again. Then she cupped both hands as if she held out a bowl. "Here's a bigger

question, then," she said. "Do you think Hawk
Woman wanted to harm Runs In Circles? Do you
think she might want to harm us?"

Kautsa was silent. She seemed to be studying
the many beads on her dress, but Kaya knew her
grandmother was pondering. After a time, she said,
"Granddaughter, this will surprise you, but there
is much that I don't know."

"You know everything!" Kaya insisted.

"Aa-heh, everything and nothing, just like anyone else," Kautsa said. She smoothed the dress and
laid it out to put on later.

Kaya waited.

"First, let me tell you what I *don't* know," Kautsa
said. "I *don't* know if Hawk Woman wanted to
harm the dog. I *don't* know if she'd harm us—but
I doubt it very much. Now let me tell you what I *do*
know. When the boys came upon Hawk Woman,
she was lost and in pain. I *do* know that Nimíipuu
have a responsibility to care for her while she's

with us, a responsibility to help her heal. We must do what we can for her, isn't that true?"

"You're wise in these things," Kaya said. "But what if we do all we can for her, and she's not even grateful?"

"Now there's a very big question. Very big!" Kautsa exclaimed, leaning forward and turning her full attention to their conversation. "You ask me, if you give a gift, shouldn't she thank you? But her gratitude, or lack of it, isn't the important thing. Have you forgotten that there's more honor in giving than in receiving?"

"I shouldn't expect thanks," Kaya admitted. "But, Kautsa, I want to help her! She only turns away. I want to be her friend, but she doesn't seem to understand friendship."

Again Kautsa was silent, thinking. "Kaya, consider this," she said after a while. "You've learned that you alone are responsible for what you do. That's true, isn't it?"

"Aa-heh, that's true," Kaya agreed.

"And you're doing your very best—isn't that also true?" Kautsa asked.

"Aa-heh, I hope so," Kaya murmured.

"So, you control what you do, but you can't control what Hawk Woman does," Kautsa went on. "That's her responsibility. Her actions are in her hands—and, remember, her hands are burned. Perhaps she's also doing the very best she can right now. Do you think that's possible?"

Now Kaya hesitated. "I'm not sure, Kautsa," she said.

Kautsa sat up straighter, her face stern, and looked directly into Kaya's eyes. "Listen to me. I want to tell you something," she said firmly.

Kaya felt her grandmother's look burning into her. When Kautsa looked at her like that, she was sending her words straight from her own heart into Kaya's.

"We all agree that Hawk Woman behaves

strangely," Kautsa said. "She goes around as if she's in a dream, looking for something we can't see. We don't understand her, and that troubles us. But we must treat her with compassion, no matter what. Others feel as I do. We agree that although her hands are healing well, her spirit is deeply wounded. A healer with very strong medicine is joining us for the Spirit Dances. We'll ask him to help Hawk Woman, to heal her spirit, if that's possible." Then she leaned forward and stroked Kaya's cheek with her warm hand. "Does that weight on your shoulders feel any lighter?" she asked in a gentler tone.

"Aa-heh, Kautsa," Kaya said. *"Katsee-yow-yow."* She took a deep breath and let it out slowly. Her heart did feel a little lighter, as it always did when she talked with her grandmother.

"Do you have any other big questions for me, or shall we help prepare the welcome dinner?" Kautsa asked. "Our visitors will begin arriving soon now."

Kaya did have another question. She wanted
to ask Kautsa if she thought Tatlo could be in any
danger from Hawk Woman's power. But she knew
that her grandmother needed to join the other
women at the cooking fires. "I think I'll always
have questions for you," she said, making her
voice lighter.

"Aa-heh, tawts!" Kautsa said. "When I was
a girl I had many questions, and do you know,
granddaughter? I still do!" She got to her feet and
looked at the cooking fire nearby. "We need more
wood or that elk meat won't cook well."

"I'll get more," Kaya said quickly. She wrapped
herself in her elk hide and took a piece of rope to
tie the driftwood. "I'll be back soon."

As Kaya walked downstream, she thought of
all that Kautsa had said. She prayed that Swan
Circling would send a sign of some kind to help
her understand what she must do now to help
Hawk Woman—and to protect Tatlo, if he needed

protection. But she saw only mist hanging over black water and heard only the hiss of snow on the pines.

chapter 7
Night of the Spirit Dances

AS THE SUN began to sink, the wind blew
harder. Kaya saw it whip the guard's elk hide as
he rode into the village with news that visitors
were approaching. Right away Toe-ta and other
men rode out to welcome them. Kaya waited by
the doorway of the longhouse to greet everyone.
Her face felt heated with excitement as she hugged
her visiting aunties and cousins and helped brush
snow from their elk hides before they came inside.
Some groups had traveled from White Bird Creek,
and others from farther downriver. They brought
news that still others from the north would arrive
the next day. Soon Kaya's longhouse was crowded
with more than thirty visitors, who were seated
at the ends and along the sides where they'd

stacked their bundles. While the men greeted one another, the boys planned races. Kaya and the girls teased each other about whose horse was the fastest. The little children were shy at first, peeping through their fingers. Light On The Water was the first to giggle, and soon the others were smiling, too.

From time to time, Kaya caught a glimpse of Hawk Woman standing near her sleeping place. She'd tucked her tattered doll into her cape, one sooty little arm sticking out, which she stroked with her fingertip.

One of Kaya's aunts, Red Duck, looked curiously at Hawk Woman. "Where does this visitor come from?" she asked Kaya.

"We're not sure, but she's dressed like the women from the seacoast," Kaya said.

"Aa-heh, I agree. Look at her cape and that lovely necklace of shells," Red Duck added. She threw Hawk Woman the words, *We welcome you.*

Hawk Woman seemed indifferent to the greeting. She was lost in her own thoughts.

Red Duck's brow furrowed in thought. "What does she call herself?" she asked Kaya.

"We don't know her name," Kaya said. "We've tried everything, but she won't talk to us."

"Perhaps she'll speak to me," Red Duck said. "One of my trading partners lives at the mouth of the Big River, and she's taught me a little of her language." She leaned forward and spoke softly and respectfully to Hawk Woman. But Hawk Woman didn't seem to understand the words. She kept her gaze on her doll.

Refusing to give up, Red Duck touched Hawk Woman's shoulder. When Hawk Woman looked up, Red Duck threw her the words, *A medicine man with strong powers traveled with us. He'll lead the Spirit Dances tonight.*

At those words Hawk Woman bit her lip and frowned. She went to sit by the doorway, her arms wrapped around her knees and her back turned to everyone.

"Does she always turn aside goodwill?" Red Duck asked with a sigh.

Kaya nodded. "We don't know how to reach her," she said. "I hope the medicine man can."

At dusk the women served the welcome meal. Afterward, all the grown-ups, and the girls and boys who had gone on their vision quests, dressed themselves in their finest clothes and crossed the clearing to the Spirit Dances longhouse. The visiting medicine man led the way, his fur headdress set with mountain-sheep horns. He carried a long cane with deer-hoof rattles tied to it. Carrying gifts for the give-away, the men followed with their heads high, their faces solemn. The women with their gifts went next. Kaya saw that although Hawk Woman hung back, Bear Blanket kept right at her side, even holding aside the door flap for her and walking into the longhouse behind her.

Not long ago, Little Fawn and Raven had gone
on their vision quests and had received wyakins,
so tonight they joined the adults for the first time.
As her older cousins entered the new lodge with
the others, Kaya watched, longing to join them.
She prayed that the time would come soon. *How
much longer must I wait?* she wondered, trying hard
to be patient until that day came.

For now, Kaya had the job of looking after
the little children for the night. They were too
young and vulnerable to be close to the dances,
where spirits would be very powerful and the
singing and dancing would be so intense. The
young ones would all sleep together in one
longhouse.

As Kaya spread hides to make beds for the
children, she was hardly aware of what she was
doing. She was listening intently to the sounds that
began to move through the night. As she helped a
little boy pull off his moccasins, she heard a man's

deep voice as he began his song. As she tucked a baby into a hide swing hung between the lodge-poles, she heard other singers take up his song with him. They kept their voices soft so that his could be heard over them all, though the wind whirled away his words.

Soon all the children had crawled under their warm buffalo hides, and the babies were asleep. Fox Tail and the other boys made themselves beds between the fires. On their side of the longhouse, Rabbit and Speaking Rain lay down, too, leaving room for Kaya beside them. But she sat awake, listening.

A wind that seemed as cold as the tinkle of icicles rustled the mats of the longhouse. Because there was no drumming, Kaya could hear the beat of the dancers' rhythmic steps on the packed earth. The steps began slowly, but soon the dancers were moving swiftly as the songs filled them with the joy of dancing. Kaya had been told that a man who got his power from an elk would raise his arms and spread his fingers to imitate antlers. She knew that other dancers with powers from deer or antelope would hold out two fingers to imitate split hooves. She imagined those who had their power from horses dancing fast and freely, galloping. She could clearly hear the medicine man rhythmically beating his cane on the ground to make the deer-hoof rattles clatter. There were other mysterious sounds now that she didn't recognize, as if the darkness were singing, too.

When all the other children slept, Kaya wrapped herself in her elk hide and stepped outside. The sky was filled with racing clouds, and as she gazed up, an opening in them appeared, a slice of clear sky showing through. Sheets of northern lights in green and gold and blue shimmered and danced in the starry sky before the clouds swept over again, leaving the night even darker than before.

As she stood shivering and sleepless, Kaya wondered if even now the medicine man was healing Hawk Woman's troubled spirit. She was determined to find out as soon as sunup came. Taking a few steps closer to the gathering, she heard an old woman with a quavering voice begin to sing. Her voice was tentative at first as she tried to coax forth her song, given to her many years ago by her wyakin. But gradually her voice grew stronger, and soon other women joined her until her song was carried by many voices. *Someday I'll sing with them,* Kaya thought. *Someday I'll have a song of my own to give the others.*

But first she must go alone to wait for her wyakin, and for that vigil she'd have to be strong, and brave, and patient. What troubled her wasn't the hardships she would endure, but the thought that maybe no wyakin would come to her. For as she listened to the singer feeding her power with her song, Kaya felt both weak and undeserving of a wyakin. She had been given so much, but maybe she'd wasted all those gifts with her bad feelings about Hawk Woman.

chapter 8
A Visit from a Wolf

AT SUNUP THE little children began to
waken. Kaya roused herself, too, though she felt
dry-eyed and tired, for her sleep had been broken
and fitful. She and Rabbit helped the little ones
dress, and Speaking Rain gave them finger cakes
to munch on. When Kaya went outside, she saw
men and women coming to the longhouses to rest
before the next night of the Spirit Dances began.
She looked for Little Fawn—she wanted to ask her
if the healer with powerful medicine had been able
to help Hawk Woman.

Little Fawn's cheeks were pale with fatigue, but
when she saw Kaya waiting, she walked quickly to
meet her.

"Tawts may-we," Kaya greeted her cousin.

"Tawts may-we," Little Fawn answered, rubbing her eyes with the heels of her hands. "Is Hawk Woman still asleep in your longhouse?"

Kaya was startled. "I thought she was with you and the others."

"Aa-heh, she was," Little Fawn said. "But she kept apart from everyone. She looked so lost, so full of grief. Bear Blanket saw her go into your longhouse and said we should let her be. She didn't come back."

Kaya glanced at the Spirit Dances longhouse. If Hawk Woman hadn't returned to the gathering, where could she have gone?

Kaya hurried to Hawk Woman's resting place. The hides she'd used were neatly folded, and the pillow Kaya had made lay on top of them. But Hawk Woman's bearskin was gone. Kaya felt under the hides—the doll was gone, too. It came to her that Hawk Woman might have left the village for good. If she had, had she taken Tatlo with her?

Kaya's pulse sped as she remembered her mother's words of counsel at Swan Circling's ceremony: "It's not good for us to mourn at night. Spirits are active then and might take us away with them."

Whistling for her dog, Kaya walked between the longhouses where most of the dogs still slept, their heads tucked into their tails. The more she searched, the more troubled she became, because Tatlo wasn't anywhere to be found. Kaya was certain now that Hawk Woman had gone away— but where was she headed? And why had she left in the dark, when spirits were so near and so strong?

Knowing she must follow, and quickly, Kaya dressed herself in her warm leggings and fur-lined moccasins. In case she might be stranded in this bitter cold, she made a bundle with some dried hemp and reed bits for fire starters, and a flint striker. She quickly told Speaking Rain that she was going in search of Hawk Woman. Then she pulled her elk-hide robe over her shoulders and walked a circle around the village. All the footprints in the fresh snow led toward the river. She went that way.

Mist blew across the swiftly moving black water. On the far side, hemlocks were filling with the snow that sailed sideways in the wind. Kaya saw footprints on the beach of those who had come here for water or to wash. She saw prints made by the village crier's horse. And prints made by a woman and a dog continued upstream and around the bend. These prints were almost filled with the fine snow that drove like needles against Kaya's face. Hawk Woman had come this way, and she hadn't bothered to conceal her trail. But if Kaya didn't follow at once, all traces of it would disappear. A staccato burst of tapping broke into her thoughts—a woodpecker was at work on a dead tree. *Get going!* the tapping said. Were the Stick People warning her to be swift? She ran.

For a while Hawk Woman's tracks followed the river. Already snow had almost erased them, and the northeast wind howled, promising more snow to come. As Kaya ran into the squall, sleet began to sting her cheeks. Bad weather was swiftly descending into the valley.

Then the tracks turned away from the shore and led into a steep draw carved into the plateau above the river. Kaya knew this was the trail that led to the camas prairie, but that was far to the north. Why would Hawk Woman head this way? Kaya ran faster, for the trail was disappearing even as she followed it.

Where the hills grew steeper, the tracks Kaya followed left the main path and joined a little game trail. Deer hooves had punched into the snow, and mountain sheep had ascended this steep crevasse, too. The trail was icy, and the going was difficult. Kaya climbed slowly, grasping roots, pulling herself around boulders. Could Hawk Woman have climbed this trail with her injured hands—and in the dark as well? If she had, surely she'd climbed slowly. Maybe she wasn't far ahead now. Kaya paused to catch her breath and get a better look at the jagged trail. As she squinted into the driving snow, she heard a shrill scream.

Kaya held her breath. The scream came again, like a woman crying out in pain. Hawk Woman? Again the scream knifed into the silence. But now Kaya realized that it wasn't a woman's voice she heard but the scream of a cougar from the valley below. Dogs usually could chase off a cougar, but a large, hungry one could attack Hawk Woman or Tatlo and kill either of them, as a cougar had killed Runs In Circles. Was Hawk Woman so intent on running away that she didn't care about her own safety, or Tatlo's? Fear and anger flooded Kaya, and her heart clenched as tight as a fist.

As she peered down the trail below, trying to get control of her breath, she felt the back of her neck prickling. All of her senses alerted, she turned slowly to look uphill again. No farther away than the length of a lodgepole, someone gazed at her from under bent-over pine branches. Who was standing there? Kaya blinked, and shielded her eyes. Then she realized that the largest wolf she'd ever seen was gazing at her through the branches and the slanting snow. Its yellow eyes, rimmed in black, watched her steadily. Its pale ears pricked toward her with curiosity. It seemed to be waiting for her. She held its gaze.

As she watched, the wolf lifted a forepaw delicately and took a single step closer over the icy rocks. It had a black scar above one eye and a rip in one ear. Its pale coat showed black guard hairs on its back and shoulders. The wolf looked old, and wise. Kaya returned its look, and it seemed to her that the wolf was saying something with its eyes.

Listen to me, Kaya heard the old wolf say. *I have something to tell you. Hawk Woman needs your help.*

"I've tried to help her," Kaya murmured, "but she always turns away from me."

Try again. You've been searching for her in anger. The old wolf looked straight into Kaya's eyes. *You must search for her with an open heart.*

"She took my dog," Kaya said very softly.

He went with her to help her. The wolf lowered its head a little, still gazing intently into Kaya's eyes. *She's lost her way in this life. You must try to lead her back. Have you heard me well?*

"Aa-heh, I've heard you well," she whispered. "Katsee-yow-yow."

The wolf looked at her a little longer, then turned and trotted slowly at an angle across the steep slope, disappearing into the snow-covered scrub pine.

Kaya stood gazing at the wolf's large paw prints, already filling with snow. She knew the old wolf was right—it wasn't Hawk Woman's fault that she was injured or that she was in despair. Kaya admitted, too, that her heart had been filled with bad feelings as she searched for Hawk Woman. But now those troubled feelings melted away and she remembered Kautsa's words: "We must treat her with compassion, no matter what." That was what Swan Circling would have done, and it was what Kaya would do now. She hurried to follow Hawk Woman's trail upward.

chapter 9

Hawk Woman's Story

THE WIND WAS a howl as Kaya climbed the steep game trail. She followed the tracks in the snow, but she often looked up at the ragged clouds, too, so that she could judge the weather. In a sheltered gully she caught sight of a great horned owl perched overhead in a pine, its mottled feathers soft and brown. Black circles surrounded pale eyes that stared steadily at her through the gusting snow. As she passed under its perch, it swiveled its head to watch her. Kaya shuddered. It was a very bad omen to see an owl in the daytime. Was the owl a warning that more dangers lay ahead?

Close to the ridgeline, wind sweeping over the top had completely erased the trail. Kaya knelt by the cliff face and spotted a bit of bearskin caught on a thorn. Hawk Woman in her bearskin robe had come this way. A little farther on Kaya saw a smudged footprint protected from the wind by a low, rocky overhang. She went to her knees, crept forward, and eased under the overhang. An opening in the rocks led into darkness. She heard a dog growl, and she cried, "Tatlo!" In a moment she felt more than saw him rush against her to lick her cheek. She pressed her face to his soft ear and tried to slow her breath. Then she crawled forward. Tatlo backed up to make room for her as she entered a small cave and got to her feet.

As her eyes adjusted to the deep gloom, Kaya made out Hawk Woman sitting huddled in her bearskin robe, holding her doll against her face. She looked up at Kaya with surprise, her hair in damp strands on her cheeks.

Kaya glanced around the cave. The roof of it was only a little higher than her head. In the

stone ceiling there was a small opening stained
by smoke. Charred sticks and ash lined a fire pit
under the opening, and some pieces of dry wood
lay by the entrance, showing that hunters sometimes sheltered here. Kaya carefully arranged the
dry wood in the fire pit, unrolled her bundle, and,
with the fire starters and the flint she'd brought,
soon had a fire going.

The little cave warmed quickly, and with the
firelight Kaya could see Hawk Woman more
clearly. Her dark eyes were filmed with unshed
tears. Now that anger didn't cloud Kaya's sight,
she realized that the woman looked tired, frightened, and very young, not at all like someone who
would do harm to anyone or anything. And Kaya
was startled to see that her hands were no longer
bandaged. Bear Blanket's medicine had healed the
burns well, but the new skin looked very pink and
very tender.

Kaya sat across the fire from Hawk Woman, and

Tatlo lay down between them, his head resting on his paws. Kaya threw Hawk Woman the words, *You found a good shelter.*

Hawk Woman's eyes brightened a little as she pointed to Tatlo—he'd led her away from the cougar and the storm to the safety of this cave.

As Kaya stroked Tatlo's head, it came to her that her dog had been a better friend to Hawk Woman than she had. She leaned toward Hawk Woman, throwing her the words, *My dog and I will go back to my village when the storm passes. Will you come?*

Hawk Woman looked from Kaya to Tatlo, then back again. She seemed to be considering whether or not she could trust Kaya.

Again Kaya threw her the words, *Will you come?* Kaya looked into Hawk Woman's eyes, urging her to believe the good intentions in her heart.

Hawk Woman bowed her head and put down the little doll, laying it across her legs. She used her hands tentatively, as if they still hurt, but she threw Kaya the words, *I will go north.*

Kaya was elated that at last Hawk Woman was able to talk with her in sign language. Quickly she signed, *You can go north with us at root-digging time.*

Hawk Woman shook her head, her face a mask of distress. *I will go north now!* she signed. As she spoke urgently with her hands, her wrist brushed against the doll, knocking it off her legs. It toppled forward and fell into the fire with a shower of sparks.

With a shriek of alarm, Hawk Woman grabbed for the doll. But Kaya had already snatched it from the flames. She slapped burning sparks from the doll's head and arms. "Here!" Kaya cried. "Here!" She thrust the doll into Hawk Woman's grasp.

Hawk Woman seized the doll, kissing it over and over. Then she yanked the bearskin forward to cover her head and began to weep violently. Her shoulders heaved, and her sobs seemed to be torn from someplace deep inside her.

Shaken by Hawk Woman's emotion, Kaya sat very still, pondering. Although the woman had always seemed sad, she'd never let the tears in her eyes fall. What had happened now to release these tears that had been hidden inside her for so long?

Hawk Woman wept on and on. Kaya waited patiently, adding another stick to the fire from time to time. At last Hawk Woman pushed the bearskin back from her head and wiped her face. Her eyes were red and swollen, but confusion seemed washed from them. Slowly, she made the sign first for *heart,* then for *know*—telling Kaya, *I remember.*

Quickly, Kaya threw her the words, *What do you remember?*

More tears coursed down Hawk Woman's cheeks as she threw Kaya the words, *A fire! I remember a fire.*

Kaya's gaze went to Hawk Woman's injured hands. *Do you remember the fire that burned you?* Kaya signed.

Hawk Woman nodded. *Lightning struck the tepee,* she signed. *Fire was everywhere!* With a groan, she bent forward, her eyes pressed closed as if she couldn't bear what she saw in her memory.

Kaya gently placed her hand on Hawk Woman's knee, and after a moment the woman opened her eyes again. *Where were you?* Kaya signed.

To the north, Hawk Woman signed. *We camped by a river. I remember that a burning tree fell into the water.*

Kaya thought a moment—Hawk Woman said *we,* but she'd been alone when the boys found her. Kaya threw her the words, *Who was with you?*

I was with my husband, Hawk Woman signed. *And my baby.*

Kaya was startled. Husband? Baby? She signed, *Where are they now?*

Hawk Woman's mouth became an O of anguish, and her eyes widened in pain. *I remember!* she signed. *Lightning killed my husband! I couldn't find my baby. Did the lightning kill her, too? My baby!* Kaya watched helplessly as the terrible scene flooded back to Hawk Woman, and again she wept.

This was much, much worse than Kaya could have imagined. As she looked into Hawk Woman's grieving face, it seemed that she'd been better off when she didn't remember the tragedy that had struck her and her family. Kaya moved around the fire to sit at her side. She put her arm over the woman's shoulders and held her close for a long time, the way Kautsa did when Kaya needed comforting.

When Hawk Woman had cried herself out a second time, she turned toward Kaya and began speaking with her hands again, signs that came in a rush. Starting, stopping, starting again, she told Kaya that some time ago warriors from up

the coast had raided her village. She was taken
captive and made a slave. Her captors took her
with them to the Big River. There, a man from over
the high mountains saw her and made her his
wife. He was a good man. She went with him and
lived with his people. She was traveling with her
husband when a storm stranded them. Lightning
hit their tepee! She beat at the fire with her hands,
trying to save her baby, her husband. Then everything went black. When she woke, she didn't know
where she was. She wandered, searching, searching for something she couldn't remember. She'd
lost her mind.

Do you understand me? she asked Kaya urgently
with her hands.

Kaya was glad she didn't need to speak, for as
Hawk Woman told her story, Kaya's throat tight-
ened with tears. *I understand you,* she signed.

Hawk Woman held the tattered doll to her
cheek again, then laid it down so she could throw

Kaya the words, *This doll was my baby's. When it fell
into the fire, the cloud in my mind disappeared. Now
I can see it all.*

Kaya sat thinking of all that Hawk Woman
had told her. The wolf had said that the woman
had lost her way in this world—and the wolf was
wise. Kaya understood now how shock and grief
had made her lose her mind, and why she couldn't
respond to those who wanted to help her. But Kaya
also knew that there would be more grief ahead for
Hawk Woman before her spirit could heal, as her
hands had, and Kaya's heart ached for her.

Tatlo got up and stretched deeply, his head
raised and his hind legs extended. They'd been
sitting in the cave for a long time. Kaya went to
the opening, crouched, and peeked out. Snow had
stopped falling, and the wind had dropped—the
storm was passing over, and travel was safer now.
Kaya threw Hawk Woman the words, *We must go
back to my village. My dog will lead us and protect us.*

Hawk Woman let her gaze rest on Tatlo, his ears pricked in eagerness to go. She stroked his head, and then she signed, *When I was out of my mind, I thought he was my husband's dog. I thought he'd sent his dog to help me.*

chapter 10

Gift From The Stick People

TATLO LED THE way. Kaya and Hawk Woman followed him down the jagged trails to the gentle slopes above the river valley. Shafts of sun struck through the gray clouds and reflected off the ice along the shore. Though the storm had ended, the day was bitterly cold. Kaya had expected to find the space around the longhouses deserted, with everyone inside near the fires. Instead, she saw some women unloading pack horses, and she realized that more visitors had arrived and were settling in.

Hawk Woman was stumbling with fatigue, so Kaya led her around the side of the hill, out of sight behind their longhouse. She went with the woman to her resting place inside Kaya's longhouse, took off her wet moccasins, and covered her with an elk hide to warm her. She hoped Hawk Woman would rest well before she encountered the others. Then Kaya went to find her grandmother—she wanted to tell Kautsa all she'd learned and ask her what they could do now for Hawk Woman.

The Spirit Dances wouldn't begin again until dark, so everyone had gathered in the other long-house to welcome the new arrivals. Kaya slipped under the door flap and found herself in a crowd. Men sat talking with the white-haired man who had just arrived, a respected elder. Women and children gathered around his wife, Yellow Sky, who sat at the far end of the longhouse. Kaya squeezed along the wall to Speaking Rain and took her hand. "I brought back Hawk Woman," she whispered to her sister.

"Aa-heh, tawts!" Speaking Rain clasped Kaya's hand. "I knew you would!"

"She told me her story," Kaya said. "I think she'll tell everyone later."

"Yellow Sky has a story to tell us, too," Speaking Rain said. "She says she has a huge surprise!"

Kaya inched forward around the women and girls until she found a place to stand beside Kautsa. She peeked over Bear Blanket's shoulder so that she could see Yellow Sky, who was seated on a pile of hides.

Yellow Sky was a thin old woman with sagging cheeks, but her face was alight as she looked around her, for she was a good storyteller and enjoyed having a new tale to share with everyone.

"You all know Crane Song," Yellow Sky said. "You know she's got three sons and a baby daughter, too."

Everyone, even the little children, murmured, "Aa-heh."

"Tawts," Yellow Sky said. "Crane Song and her family were heading downriver to her husband's people when we met them on the trail. We stopped to rest a bit and visit with them. I asked Crane

Song about her baby, and she went to get her. When she came back, she brought me a big surprise, as I've said!"

"Let's hear about this surprise quickly," Bear Blanket urged her old friend. "I've lived a long time and seen many new things. Maybe what surprised you won't surprise me at all."

Yellow Sky fixed her dark eyes on Bear Blanket. "When you were a child, you were impatient, too!" she said with a laugh.

"Aa-heh! But now I'm old," Bear Blanket said. "And maybe my hearing will be gone before you finish your story!"

Yellow Sky rolled her eyes. "Let me tell you what happened. Crane Song came to me with a tee-kas in her arms, and in the tee-kas was her beautiful baby. 'Ah!' I said to her. 'She's a precious one!' Crane Song smiled with pride. Then she handed the baby to her sister, and in a moment she came to me again, carrying another baby in another tee-kas! I thought I was seeing double, and I blinked. No, it wasn't my sight—there were two babies! 'I didn't know you had twins!' I said to Crane Song. 'I don't have twins,' she said. 'This other baby was given to us by the Stick People!'" Yellow Sky paused, waiting for everyone to take in this news.

Bear Blanket snorted. "That doesn't surprise me at all," she insisted. "The Stick People give us many things."

"Wait, there's more," Yellow Sky said. "Let me tell you how it all happened."

Bear Blanket snorted again, but Kaya saw that she leaned closer to make sure she wouldn't miss a word. Kaya leaned forward, too.

"Crane Song told me that they were coming down from the high country just ahead of the snows," Yellow Sky said. "Forest fires from light-ning strikes still burned here and there. They had to travel carefully to avoid them. They were coming

along the trail by the river when they heard a
baby crying. They thought another hunting party
was nearby, but there was no one in sight, and no
camp, either. Then they rode around the bend and
came upon a baby in a tee-kas, propped against a
tamarack. The baby was howling with hunger, face
all red! Right away Crane Song unlaced the tee-
kas, cleaned the baby, and fed her while the men
searched for her parents."

"Did they find any sign of them?" Kautsa asked
in a worried tone.

Yellow Sky sighed, the creases around her eyes
deepening. "Crane Song said that the men found
a burned tepee, smoke still rising from the ashes.
There was a man's body there, and the bodies of
his horses—all killed by lightning. They searched
hard for the woman's body, but there was no sign
of it. Maybe a bear dragged it off. They had to
keep moving to stay ahead of the coming snows,
so they broke off the search and buried the man.

Only the baby was alive."

"That baby was very, very fortunate to be saved," Bear Blanket said in a low voice.

Yellow Sky nodded. "Crane Song said it was the Stick People who saved the baby's life. They're strong, you know! She says they carried the baby away from the fire and put her beside the trail so travelers could find her and care for her. She named the baby Gift From The Stick People, and she thanked them with many gifts."

As she listened, Kaya's heart raced, though she tried not to let her thoughts run too quickly. The fire, the burned tepee, and the baby—Crane Song's story matched Hawk Woman's. Was it possible that the gift baby was Hawk Woman's lost child? Kaya cautioned herself to learn more before she raised Hawk Woman's hopes. "Yellow Sky, what does the gift baby's tee-kas look like?" she asked respectfully.

Yellow Sky fixed her sharp gaze on Kaya. "I can

see you've got a good mind," she said, "because
that tee-kas is part of my story. It's not made like
ours. It's made of cedar, with cedar-bark cloth for
a wrapping. Women from the coast make their
tee-kas like that, and the baby has a pretty necklace
of dentalium shells. Why her unfortunate parents
were traveling in Nimíipuu country is a mystery,
but she's safe now in Crane Song's care."

Kaya moved back until she could stand beside
Kautsa again. "I think the baby's mother could be
alive!" she whispered at her grandmother's ear.

Kautsa turned to look closely at Kaya. "Why do
you say that, granddaughter?"

"Hawk Woman's memory came back," Kaya
whispered. "She told me that lightning struck her
tepee and set it on fire, with her family inside it. As
she tried to beat out the flames, she was knocked
unconscious. When she came to her senses again,
her husband was dead and her baby was gone. She
went out of her mind then and began wandering.

Don't you think that gift baby could be hers?"

Kautsa showed no emotion as she listened, but Kaya knew that the more excited her grandmother was on the inside, the quieter she became on the outside. She waited to hear what Kautsa would say next.

"This is a very strange coincidence, but I've known stranger things," Kautsa said after a little thought. "If you get your horse, do you think you could catch up with Crane Song and her family on the river trail?"

"Steps High is as swift as the wind!" Kaya said. "I'm sure I can catch them!"

"Tawts," Kautsa said. "You must be the one to go, Kaya. You can tell them all that you've learned. And urge them to come here with you. Only Hawk Woman will know if the baby is hers. Be on your way!"

...

It was almost dusk when Kaya returned to her village accompanied by Crane Song and her family. Both women and men came to greet them and help them with the horses. Kaya ran to the longhouse where Hawk Woman had her sleeping place. She found the woman curled on her side under the elk hide. Her eyes were closed, but Kaya could tell from the woman's shallow, labored breathing that she'd wakened from her exhausted sleep. Kaya grabbed a pair of dry moccasins from her parfleche and knelt by the woman, putting her hand on her shoulder. When Hawk Woman turned to her, Kaya threw her the words, *Put these on and come with me.*

Like a tired but obedient child, Hawk Woman sat up and did as she was told, then wrapped a deer hide around her shoulders and followed Kaya across the clearing to the other longhouse. If she noticed visitors carrying in their bundles, she didn't say. She walked with slow steps, like a woman carrying a heavy load with a long way to go before she could put it down.

Kaya pulled aside the door flap, but Hawk Woman stepped back when she saw the crowd inside. Kaya took her hand firmly and led her forward.

Kautsa must have told the others what Kaya had said, for everyone opened a way for Hawk Woman, looking at her expectantly as she passed. Crane Song held out her hand to Hawk Woman, beckoning her to come close to where she sat, holding the baby in its tee-kas.

Kaya held her breath as Hawk Woman stepped forward hesitantly to gaze down at the baby. Then, with a gasp, she sank to her knees and took the baby's round face in her trembling hands. She murmured something as she looked into the dark eyes shining up at her, and she began kissing the baby's cheeks over and over. Her tears overflowed as she turned her questioning gaze back to Kaya.

Crane Song found her by the trail, Kaya signed. *She's treated her like her own child.*

Hawk Woman threw Crane Song the words, *Thank you!* She signed, *katsee-yow-yow!* to Kaya, too, and to Bear Blanket, and Kautsa, and Little Fawn, and all the others gathered around.

As Kaya watched Hawk Woman unlace the tee-kas ties and lovingly kiss each of her baby's plump toes, her heart rejoiced, and she was sure that Swan Circling's spirit rejoiced, too.

chapter 11

Hawk Rising

IN THE MORNING, when Kaya left the longhouse, the snowy hills shone and sparkled in the early sun. It was rare to have this much snow here in Salmon River Country, and all the children wanted to play in it. Fox Tail and other boys were strapping on snowshoes so that they could have races. Rabbit was helping some little girls make snow people with pebbles for eyes and twigs for arms. Other children were sliding down the slopes on sleds made of buffalo ribs laced together with strips of rawhide. Dogs chased the sleds, barking and tossing snow with their noses. Shouts and laughter echoed off the hills around the village.

With a sled under her arm, Kaya walked with

her little brothers to the bottom of the sledding hill. "Who'll make the first run on this sled?" she asked them.

"I'll go first!" Wing Feather cried.

"We can ride down together," Sparrow insisted.

"Aa-heh, together," Wing Feather agreed.

"Tawts! Then pull the sled together, too," Kaya said, handing the boys the sled line. They grasped it and started up the hill. Tatlo dashed ahead, only to turn and come leaping back again as if urging them on. As Kaya trudged up behind the boys, she smiled at her big, strong-hearted dog, and it seemed to her that he smiled back.

At the top of the slope, Kaya turned the sled around. "Sparrow, you lie on your belly," she said. "Wing Feather, you lie on top of your brother and guide the sled. Remember, drag your feet to slow down."

"We don't want to slow down!" cried Wing Feather as he pushed off, then flung himself onto

Sparrow's back as the sled began sailing down the hill.

Arms folded, Kaya watched the twins on the sled speeding over the snow, with Tatlo running alongside. If the sled overturned, the soft snow would cushion them, and in a little while they'd be climbing the hill again to make more runs with the others.

Kaya thought she should be enjoying the games around her, but something pricked in her throat as if she had swallowed a fish bone. What was troubling her?

Surely she'd done all she could for Hawk Woman. Before the Spirit Dances began last night, she'd made sure everyone understood that Hawk Woman had found her memory again and that she was a woman to be trusted. She'd assured Hawk Woman that when they went to the Big River, they'd find traders from the coast to take her back to her own people. During last night's dances,

Hawk Woman had stayed in the children's lodge so she could be with her baby, and Kaya saw that for the first time she slept peacefully. *Swan Circling, is there some further help I need to give?* Kaya beseeched her friend's spirit.

As Kaya pondered this question, she watched Tatlo and the twins wrestle and romp in the snow at the foot of the hill. Then another thought came to her as clearly as if Swan Circling had whispered it in her ear. Leaving the twins to their fun with the other children, she headed back to the longhouse.

Kaya found Hawk Woman seated at her resting place, putting fresh cattail fluff underneath her baby, who was waving her arms and kicking her plump legs in the air. Hawk Woman looked up at Kaya with a wide smile, throwing her the words, *She's a healthy girl! Crane Song cared for her well.*

"Aa-heh," Kaya agreed, sitting beside Hawk Woman and giving the baby's foot a squeeze. Then

Kaya threw Hawk Woman the words, *What do you call yourself?*

I call myself Hawk Rising, the woman signed.

"Aa-heh, tawts!" Kaya exclaimed, for her guess about the woman's name was a good one. *I call myself She Who Arranges Rocks,* she signed. "Kaya'aton'my'," she said aloud.

"Kaya'aton'my'," Hawk Rising repeated.

Kaya sat watching Hawk Rising bundle her baby into the tee-kas again, her face glowing with happiness. When the baby was laced in snugly, Kaya threw the woman the words, *I want to tell you something.*

Hawk Rising nodded.

Soon you will go back to your people, Kaya signed. *When you go, I want you to take Tatlo. He will protect you. He will protect your baby. I want him to be your dog now.* Then she took a deep breath—she felt at peace giving Tatlo to the woman who had needed him so much, as Swan Circling wanted her to do.

Hawk Rising's dark eyes met Kaya's, and she put her hand on her heart. She threw Kaya the words, *Katsee-yow-yow.*

When Hawk Rising turned back to her baby, Kaya got to her feet. She looked around and saw her grandmother standing just inside the door opening. Kautsa beckoned to Kaya and walked beside her as they stepped out into the bright morning.

"Granddaughter, I must tell you something," Kautsa said gently. "I was mistaken."

"Mistaken?" Kaya asked. "Mistaken about what?"

Kautsa placed her hand firmly on Kaya's shoulder and looked down into her eyes. "I was mistaken about you," Kautsa said. "I thought you loved your dog as a child would, too attached to him to give him up. But when I saw you give Tatlo to Hawk Rising, I realized you've become a young woman. I think it's time now for you to take Swan Circling's name. And as soon as warm weather returns, it's time for you to go on your vision quest to meet your wyakin and find the good trail. Are you ready for these things, granddaughter?"

Kaya seized her grandmother's hand in hers. Her racing heart swelled with gratitude for Kautsa's understanding, and with anticipation for all that lay ahead. "Aa-heh, I'm ready, Kautsa!" she whispered.

Inside Kaya's World

A Nez Perce girl like Kaya had close ties to everyone in her village. They were people she had known all her life. They shared their work and their food, their hardships and celebrations. They depended on one another for survival, and they each knew that their individual actions affected the well-being of the entire village.

The arrival of a stranger would spark great curiosity—and also unease, especially if he or she didn't know the Nez Perce language or sign language. And a newcomer who didn't know Nez Perce customs might seem impolite or unfriendly without meaning to be. Kaya's elders realized this, and they wisely cautioned Kaya not to jump to conclusions about Hawk Woman, despite her odd behavior.

A stranger traveling alone, like Hawk Woman, would be especially worrying. Indians almost always traveled in groups so that if someone got injured or sick, others could help. A lone traveler usually meant that something bad had happened. For example, Hawk Woman might have been banished from her village—the harshest punishment that a tribe could impose. Or, as Kaya's grandmother Kautsa speculated, perhaps Hawk Woman had been enslaved by another tribe and was running away from her captors.

Even though nobody knew what had happened to

Hawk Woman, everyone could see that she was deeply disturbed—and this added to their worry, because the Nez Perce believed that a person with a troubled spirit could bring misfortune to others. This danger would be especially strong during the winter Spirit Dances. At that time, people's *wyakins,* or guardian spirits, drew close to their human partners, and all spirits, both good and bad, became more powerful. Even if the stranger meant no harm, she might still bring trouble to the village.

When Hawk Woman arrived, the *shaman,* Bear Blanket, examined her. A shaman, or healer, was a respected man or woman who had great knowledge of healing plants and rituals, and also deep insight into human nature and spiritual matters. Bear Blanket was like a doctor who could treat illnesses of the body, mind, and spirit.

Although Kaya's people worried that Hawk Woman might bring harm to their village, they treated her with compassion. The Nez Perce—and many other Native American tribes—placed great value on hospitality. The people in Kaya's village knew that without their help, Hawk Woman would probably not survive. Even though they weren't sure whether they could trust her, they believed that helping a stranger was the right thing to do.

GLOSSARY
of Nez Perce Words

In the story, Nez Perce words are spelled so that English readers can pronounce them. Here, you can also see how the words are actually spelled and said by the Nez Perce people.

PHONETIC/ NEZ PERCE	PRONUNCIATION	MEANING
aa-heh/´éehe	*AA-heh*	yes, that's right
Eetsa/Iice	*EET-sah*	mother
katsee-yow-yow/ qe´ci´yew´yew´	*KAHT-see-yow-yow*	thank you
Kautsa/Qáaca´c	*KOUT-sah*	grandmother from mother's side
Kaya´aton´my´	*ky-YAAH-a-ton-my*	she who arranges rocks
Nimíipuu	*nee-MEE-poo*	The People; known today as the Nez Perce
Tatlo	*TAHT-lo*	ground squirrel
tawts/ta´c	*TAWTS*	good
tawts may-we/ ta´c méeywi	*TAWTS MAY-wee*	good morning

tee-kas/tikée´s	*tee-KAHS*	baby board, or cradleboard
Toe-ta/Toot´a	*TOH-tah*	father
wapalwaapal	*WAH-pul-WAAH-pul*	western yarrow, a plant that helps stop bleeding
wyakin/ wéeyekin	*WHY-ah-kin*	guardian spirit

Read more of KAYA'S stories,

available from booksellers and at *americangirl.com*

❖ *Classics* ❖

Kaya's classic series, now in two volumes:

Volume 1:
The Journey Begins
Kaya, her sister, and her horse
are captured! If Kaya escapes,
will she ever see Speaking Rain
and Steps High again?

Volume 2:
Smoke on the Wind
As Kaya searches for her
lost sister and beloved horse,
a forest fire threatens all she
holds dear.

❖ *Journey in Time* ❖

Travel back in time—and spend a day with Kaya!

The Roar of the Falls

What is it like to live in Kaya's world? Ride bareback, sleep in
a tepee, and help Kaya train a filly—but watch out for bears!
Choose your own path through this multiple-ending story.

❖ *Mysteries* ❖

Enjoy more thrilling adventures with BeForever characters.

Danger in Paris
Samantha and Nellie discover a dark side to the "City of Light."

The Puzzle of the Paper Daughter
A note written in Chinese leads Julie on a search for a long-lost doll.

Shadows on Society Hill
Addy's new home holds dangerous secrets—ones that lead straight
back to the plantation she escaped from only two years before.

A Sneak Peek at

The Roar
of the Falls

My Journey with Kaya

Meet Kaya and take an unforgettable journey
in a book that lets *you* decide what happens.

I open my eyes. Bright sunlight makes me blink. My bedroom is gone, and I'm sprawled on a patch of damp grass somewhere outside. I push myself up out of the mud and stand up slowly, dizzy from all the spinning. I can't quite believe what I see. A broad river rushes by, feeding a giant waterfall, bigger than any I've ever seen. The water crashes over black rocks and fills my ears with its roar. On both sides of the water, the grassy riverbanks are covered with hundreds of shelters. Some look like tepees, and others are huts in different shapes and sizes. They stretch as far down the river as I can see. Steep bluffs rise behind me. Footpaths meander up the sides of the bluffs, and at the top, I can see horses grazing on the flatlands.

I'm no longer wearing striped pajamas. Instead, I have on some kind of brown leather dress that's decorated with delicate white shells. Fringe hangs from the front and along the hem. Lace-up leather

moccasins wrap around my feet and calves.
I recognize only one thing: the shell bracelet on
my wrist.

My heart is pounding in my chest. Where
am I? What just happened? *Don't panic*, I tell myself.
I close my eyes and take five long, slow breaths.
When I open my eyes, I'm still next to the roaring
river, but I feel a bit calmer. Wherever I am, I can't
just stand here in the mud. My damp moccasins
slide as I make my way carefully along the riverbank. There's a steep drop to the water below, and
I'm still a little dizzy.

I see people in the distance. Their clothes are
like mine, and everyone has deep brown skin and
dark hair, which they wear in two braids—even the
boys. I realize that the people look like the pictures
of American Indians I've seen in my school text-
books. *How is this possible?* I wonder as a group of
children run past with what look like toy bows and
arrows. Am I—could I be—in another time?

The overpowering roar of the waterfall makes my head ache. I'm confused and my legs are weak. I stumble, going down to my knees. I've strayed too close to the steep edge. Suddenly, the ground gives way beneath me and I'm slipping down the river-bank. Desperately, I cry out, clutching loose rocks and soil, sliding toward the crashing water below.

❖

Someone catches my arm. "Hold my hand!" a voice cries. I look up to see a girl's face above me. She clutches my wrist and pulls, and I claw my way back up the bank. Panting, I collapse on the soft grass.

"Thank you," I gasp, pushing myself up to my knees. The girl takes my arm and helps me to my feet.

I stare at the girl in wonder. She looks about my age, with black braids that reach almost to her waist and dark almond-shaped eyes that twinkle. She wears a leather dress, too, with fringes like mine, and the same moccasins.

She's staring back at me with concern. "Your face and arms are scraped," she says. "You're covered in mud, too. I'll help you get cleaned up. Where is your family's camp?"

"Camp?" I say tentatively.

The girl sweeps her arm over the clusters of shelters spread along the riverbank. "Your camp is with the rest of the *Nimíipuu*, isn't it?"

"*Nimíipuu?*" I ask. It seems like I should know what that means, but I don't.

"Of course you're *Nimíipuu*—we speak the same language." She looks at me curiously. "But we've never met," she continues.

"I—I don't really know what's happened," I stammer. It's impossible to think over the roar of the falls and the strange twist of events. I don't want to lie, but I don't think I should tell this girl that I was transported here from my bedroom.

"I just—found myself here," I say truthfully.

The girl takes my arm. "You have been frightened by your fall. You are confused. Come to my camp with me. It's not far from here. My grandmother will know what to do." The girl's brow is knit with concern. "I'm Kaya," she adds.

"Kaya," I repeat, my voice filled with gratitude. "You saved my life!" I look down the crumbled section of riverbank to the crashing, foaming water below. My stomach flops over with a nauseating twist. "That was so courageous. You could have fallen, too!"

Kaya cocks her head to one side. "*Nimíipuu* always look out for each other. That's what my grandmother says." She takes my hand and squeezes it. I can feel how strong she is.

I try not to look shocked. This girl just risked her own life to help a total stranger and now she's acting like it's not that big a deal. Does this happen all the time around here? Do people just swoop in and pluck one another from danger?

The reality of my strange situation crashes over me once more. Where is my family? Where is my home? Where am I? I sink down onto a nearby rock, trying to sort out my swimming thoughts.

"Are you unwell?" Kaya asks. "Perhaps you hit your head when you slipped. I could get Bear Blanket—she's a healer." She turns as if to run.

"No, wait." I reach out and catch Kaya's hand before she dashes off. "It's not my head. I—I—" What I really need is a chance to think for a moment alone. "Maybe just a drink of water."

Kaya pats my shoulder. "I will get water. Rest here." She dashes down the path toward the shelters.

As she disappears, I slide off the rock and onto the ground on the other side so that I'm shielded from the path. I need to be alone. I need to think. First I was in my bedroom. I was sitting on the bed. I had made this bracelet. I look down at my wrist.

Right before this thing happened, I had just put it on. Then I was touching the shell, just like this. I trace a circle around the rim of the shell with one finger and suddenly, I'm spun dizzily, whirling again, the world in blackness.

❖

I land with a thump on something soft and fuzzy and open my eyes. I'm lying on the carpet in my bedroom, wearing my pajamas. My jewelry-making things are spread out by my bed, right where I left them. The roar of the falls is gone. Instead, I can hear my father practicing scales down in the living room. The phone is ringing in my mom's study. Everything is just as it was when I left. It seems to be the same moment I left.

Have I been in another world? I know I was wearing a leather dress. I met a girl named Kaya. But now I'm back in my own room, and no time has passed. I'm wearing my own clothes again, and there are no signs of scrapes on my arms or face.

I look down at the bracelet on my wrist. Whatever is happening, the bracelet's doing it. Well, I'm doing it. I sent myself to that other world when I rubbed the shell, and that's how I got home. I could do it again!

Kaya's flashing eyes and friendly smile swim up in front of me. I'm surprised to realize that I want to leave the comfortable familiarity of my room and get to know the girl who saved my life.

Excitement seizes me as I place my fingertip on the shell. Holding my breath, I trace a circle around its edge. Once again, the room spins around me. I close my eyes, and when I open them, I'm on the grass, sitting behind the big rock, wearing the same muddy dress and damp moccasins. I'm back! But I can get home—as long as I have this bracelet.

Each night when JANET SHAW was a
girl, she took out a flashlight and book
hidden under her pillow and read until she
fell asleep. She and her brother liked to act
out stories, especially ones about sword
fights and wild horses. Today, Ms. Shaw
has three grown children. When they were
small, she often pulled them in a big red
wagon to the library, where they filled the
wagon with so many books, they had to walk
back home. Today, Ms. Shaw lives in North
Carolina with her husband and their dog.

About the Advisory Board

American Girl extends its deepest appreciation
to the advisory board that authenticated Kaya's stories.